Improvisations on a Missing String

The University of Arkansas Press Award
for
Arabic Literature in Translation
1996

Improvisations on a Missing String

NAZIK SABA YARED

Translated from the Arabic by Stuart A. Hancox

The University of Arkansas Press

Fayetteville   1997

01   00   99   98   97   5   4   3   2   1

Designed by Alice Gail Carter

Library of Congress Cataloging-in-Publication Data
Yārid, Nāzik Sābā.
    [Taqāsīm ' alá watar ḍā 'i'. English]
    Improvisations on a missing string / Nazik
Saba Yared : translated from the Arabic by
Stuart A. Hancox.
        p.   cm.
    ISBN 1-55728-495-4 (cloth : alk. paper). —
ISBN 1-55728-496-2 (paper : alk. paper).
    I. Hancox, Stuart A., 1960–   .   II. Title.
PJ7874.A77T3713   1997
892.7'36—DC21   97-36782
                                CIP

Preface

Nazik Saba Yared (b. 1928) is an accomplished author and academic, a professor of Arabic literature at the Lebanese American University in Beirut, and has to date published nine critical works and six novels. Yared's nonfiction publications range from classical to modern with critical studies on the poetry of Abu Nawas, Ibn al-Rumi, Ahmad Shauqi, Elias Abu Shabaka, Hammad Ajrad, and Gibran Kahlil Gibran. One work, based on Yared's Ph.D. thesis, a study of the intellectual and cultural conflict experienced by Christian and Arab travelers to the West, has been published in English language translation as *Arab Travelers and the West* (Dar al-Saqi, London, 1996). As to her fiction, Yared has published six novels: *Nuqtat ad-Dā'ira* (Center of the circle), 1983; *As-Sadā al-Makhnūq* (The strangled echo), 1986, which has been translated into German; *Kāna al-Ams Ghadan* (Yesterday was tomorrow), 1988; *Taqāsīm 'alaWatar Ḍā'i'a*, 1992 (*Improvisations on a Missing String,* University of Arkansas Press, 1997); *Fi Dhill al-Qal'a* (In the shadow of the citadel), 1996; and *Dhikrayāt Mulghā* (Canceled memories), 1997.

According to Miriam Cooke's classification, Yared is considered a Beirut Decentrist, "a group of young women writers who have shared Beirut as their home and the war as their experience."* Among their ranks are Ghada al-Samman, Hanan al-Shaikh, Emily Nasrallah, Laila Usairan, Daisy al-Amir, Claire Gebeyli, and Etel Adnan. A growing number of their novels, short stories, and poetry in translation is

---

*Miriam Cooke, *War's Other Voices: Women Writers on the Lebanese Civil War,* (Cambridge University Press, 1988), 3.

attracting increasing interest from both western readers and critics. Of her fiction Yared says, "I write about the things that touch Lebanese life and society," often using the Lebanese Civil War, a war that tore apart the fabric of society, as a backdrop to her novels.

Improvisations on a Missing String portrays the struggle of a Christian Arab woman, Saada Rayyis, as she attempts to find a place in the world on her own terms in the face of bias and prejudice in their myriad forms. The novel follows the life of Saada from her early reminiscences as a young girl, intelligent and academically gifted but jealous of her more attractive and popular younger sister Suha, through her later life as a high school teacher striving to succeed on a personal and professional level in the midst of the material and psychological attrition of the civil war. While on one level the novel is the portrait of a woman who is unwilling to compromise in order to achieve independence, on another it is a work of broad thematic complexity and texture in its exploration of language, literature, art, and issues and topics highly relevant within the framework of social, political, and cultural discourse on the contemporary Middle East: identity, allegiance, religion, nationalism, colonialism, pan-Arabism.

Saada, the main protagonist, is the focal point around which the narrative unfolds as she lies on a hospital bed recuperating from an operation. Through episodic flashbacks we learn of Saada's life, her choices, her mistakes, her troubled relationships with her sister and mother, the sense of disappointment over failed romances that haunts her memories, but above all we can discern a unity of purpose in the mind of a woman who has adopted a positive role in bettering her own life and the lives of others, at times to the detriment of her own emotional well-being.

Improvisations on a Missing String

The nurse opened the door a crack and gazed at the bed in front of her. *Her eyes are closed. Has she been asleep since 7:00 P.M., or is she pretending?* She tiptoed in and stood near the bed, watching her closely. *Her frail hands perfectly still on top of the bedsheet—they seem so pale, the blue veins so puffy and swollen. Her face haggard, translucent, and the cheekbones so prominent above sunken hollows which, perhaps only recently, were two plump cheeks . . . Maybe even rosy?* Suddenly the thin lips moved, a slight smile dancing upon them. *Is she asleep or just pretending?* The nurse placed a hand lightly on the frail hands and whispered, "Sitt Saada?"

The patient opened her eyes for a second, then closed them. The nurse walked over to the window and gently drew back the curtains, addressing the patient behind her, "It's a splendid day. I'm just going to let some sun in."

A wide ray fell across the bed and the frail hands, their pale skin reflecting its light and warmth. The patient opened her eyes again and peered at the nurse, who turned around and said with a smile, "See, the heat of the sun can even bring a stone back to life!"

"So I'm a *stone,* am I?"

At last a reply! They had tried to talk to her, to question her, challenge her, even provoke her. But it had been no use. It was as if she were a stone. The nurse laughed, "Of course not! I only wanted to stress how important the sun is. Breakfast is ready. I'll bring it to you right away."

She went out. *At last, alone. All by herself. Who are all these people who come to see her? She doesn't know them, nor does she want to know them. A strange place, strange people.*

The nurse came back, carrying a breakfast tray. She placed it on the bedside table, then bent down and turned the crank, raising the upper half of the bed. As she arranged the pillows behind the patient's back, she said, "I'll help you drink your tea and milk before it gets cold. I'll even spread butter and jam on the bread and cut it up for you, but you'll have to eat it by yourself."

࿐

"Take it easy on the bread and the butter, Saada. Don't you see how fat you're getting?"

"Mind your own business. It's okay for you; you're as beautiful as Mama. Leave me alone!"

Suha stopped talking. Would I be prettier if I were slim? I'm ugly, ugly, ugly . . . Mama would like to forget me. She's always out somewhere.

I came back with Suha from school at four: "Where's Mama?"

"At the hospital, visiting Najla," the maid replied.

"Najla who?"

"Why, Saad, the carpenter's daughter."

"Couldn't she have visited her before noon? Today it's Najla. Yesterday it was the widow Afeefa, and . . ."

"Saada! Your mother devotes her life to the poor and needy!"

"I wish she would devote it to me!"

"Don't be rude!"

I just didn't understand Mama. Our neighbor was a lazy drunk. Mama helped his wife find work, sent his children to public school and bought them books and school uniforms. Another neighbor, whose husband had left her, had gotten sick. I went with Mama to her small room, the woman sleeping on a mattress without sheets, covered only with a torn blanket. Three filthy children were playing with an aluminum plate and spoon on a mat littered with rice and bits of moldy bread. Mama offered the children the chocolate she had brought with her and sat down on the sick woman's bed, talking to

4

her with a great deal of sympathy. As for me, I stayed by the door disgusted, afraid of getting my clothes dirty if I sat on the only chair in the room. Class consciousness?

One day I came back from school and told my mother enthusiastically, "I think I've found a friend at last. A girl like me who doesn't care about clothes and loves books. Afaf Zand." Suddenly her expression changed: "Zand? The laundryman Zand's daughter?" I retorted angrily, "I don't know. What has her father got to do with it? So what if he's a laundryman!" But I had to obey her; she banned my "friend" before I even really got to know her. I couldn't understand my mother's inconsistent attitude: she associated with the poor and needy, yet she forbade me to make friends with a girl whose father was a laundryman? I only understood afterwards why we make friends from our own class, but the others we pity and help.

Mama was tall, slender. Her coal-black hair accentuated her pale skin and green, almond eyes. She was a queen. And when age began to streak her black tresses with gray, it only made her more majestic.

Again my hand reached out for the French bread. I cut another slice, buttered it, and stuffed it into my mouth. My hand reached out for another slice, and it immediately got slapped,

"That's enough, Saada. You're not a child anymore!"

My face burned with shame, with anger.

"It's easy for you to preach! You can eat whatever you want and don't put on any weight!"

"I don't eat as much as you do!"

Suha got up and locked up the bread in the cabinet. Angry, I ran off to my room, slamming the door behind me. They hate me, they hate me. They're trying to starve me. Food—my one pleasure! I felt the saliva gathering in my mouth, covering the inside of my cheeks, my tongue, the back of my throat—the taste of butter and apricot jam, the bread and the fruit's tartness softening the sweetness of the sugar. And eating, how could I not love it! . . . But them? Her? How I loved her! When I was a child I used to hide behind the closet, watching her secretly as she got ready to go out: she would turn around in front of the mirror, checking her dress, straightening the line of her stockings, putting back a strand of hair that had fallen out of place. She would sit down to apply eyeliner, put on rouge, lipstick. My eyes would follow her lips as she pressed them together, back and forth, filling in the red outline her hand had drawn so exactly. And when the fragrance of Parfum des Anges, her favorite perfume, tickled my nostrils, I felt that I was the happiest child on the face of the earth, a child with an angel for a mother . . .

I did not remain a child, and I lost my angel.

෫

"This is your daughter? Bless her heart!"

I never understood the looks of disbelief on the faces of the people my mother introduced me to.

"Your daughter? She doesn't look like you!"

"Maybe she looks like her father?"

"Not at all. Her aunt."

"Girls take after their aunts," the woman said.

"But I take after Mama!" I replied.

Everybody laughed, so I ran out to the garden and sat on the wooden swing, swinging and swinging, up and down, up and down, higher and higher. The wind tousled my long black hair, played against my bare legs. I reached the lowest branches of the pine, then those half-way up the tree. I leaned my body forward, bent my legs back under the swing, then shot them forward. The swing soared upwards. Eventually I was peering down on the trees from above. Was there anyone like me? I felt a surge of joy, the same kind of joy I felt when I ate Hamd's ice cream, especially if it had pistachios or almonds in it. Papa used to go to Hamd's every Saturday by taxi so that he could get home before the ice cream melted, that is until a public transportation strike brought the town to a standstill. Then Papa walked home with the ice cream. He arrived puffing and panting, circles of sweat showing on his jacket, sweat trickling down the lines on his face. The ice cream was streaming from a sack full of soggy cardboard containers floating in a milky soup of pistachios and almonds. From then on I hated ice cream.

And my mother? . . .

"Saada, Suha, I want to introduce you to a childhood friend of mine."

My sister and I went into the living room.

"Widad, these are my daughters . . . Widad was my best friend in school before she went to live in Brazil with her family. I haven't seen her for twenty years!"

When Widad hugged and kissed me, I was overcome by her heady and invigorating perfume. I felt that my mother had made a good choice in a friend like this.

"You can go back to your homework now."

We left. I shuffled into the next room to pick out a novel from my parents' book collection. As my eyes roamed the bookshelves, I heard my mother laugh, then Widad say, "If only she looked more like you, or her sister even!"

My hand froze against the bookshelf. Mama replied, "But she's intelligent. She can keep studying, enter some profession so she won't need a husband to provide for her."

Was *I* the subject of that conversation? Without taking a book, I hurried to my room, opened the closet, and stood before the mirror, examining my reflection: medium height, slightly plump; sleek black hair gathered in two braids; olive complexion; small, dark, sparkling eyes; a small, snubby nose; an average-sized mouth with full lips. I had never examined myself in such detail before. It had never occurred to me that one day I might ask myself, "Am I beautiful? Ugly? Plain?" So I was ugly. Sitt Widad thought I was ugly. Mama thought I was ugly. I scrutinized the image reflected in the mirror: my ugly face; my short, fat, ugly body. Saada! Did they choose that name because I was ugly, ugly from the day I was born? Papa told me,

"It's the name of my one and only sister. She doesn't have any children." My friends, classmates: Layla, Nuha, Muna, Huda, Ayeda. My sister: Suha. But me: Saada. Did Papa ever hear them making fun of me at school, chanting in the playground, "Saada the monkey, she hops around the pantry"? I hated my name, I hated my aunt because of that name, and I now hated myself. The right name for the right person!

"What are you doing?"

Suha's voice startled me. I quickly closed the closet door.

"I was seeing if I should let down the hem of my skirt," I lied.

Did she notice me blushing? She gave the skirt hem a fleeting glance, then said, "I don't think you've really grown that much since last year."

Yet another stab at me. Then she asked, "Can you fix my hair?"

She handed me a velvet ribbon, green like her eyes, like Mama's eyes. I gathered the waves of silky, chestnut hair in one hand, put one end of the ribbon between my teeth, and, grabbing the other end, started winding the ribbon around the bunch of hair. I tied it and started to pull harder and harder. I wished she were dead!

"Ouch! Have you gone crazy?"

But she stayed perfectly still so it wouldn't hurt even more.

"I'm only trying to make it tight so it won't slip."

As soon as I had tied the last knot, she turned to look at herself in the mirror. She took in her slim figure, her long, slender neck, her attractive features, green eyes, and upturned nose.

"Where are you going?" I said, not even trying to hide my burning curiosity.

"To Najwa's birthday party."

"Aren't the bunch of you sick of all those dumb parties?"

Before she could reply, I added, "Dumb like you!"

I left the room—I didn't want to hear anymore of her comments. I wished she had been struck dead right then and there.

∞

I'm seven years old. Papa didn't have a car, so when Uncle pulled up at our house in a brand new metallic blue sedan, we all rushed outside to look it over. We tried the door handles and the windshield wipers and tested the fenders to see how strong they were. The grown-ups went back into the house while Suha and I played by the car. I challenged her, "Let's race."

"You're bigger than me. You'll beat me."

A thought struck me: "When Uncle gets into the car, hold onto the back. It'll help you run faster."

Did I realize what I was saying, or was I just naive and actually believed it? I don't know. All I remember is that when Uncle got in the car, he didn't see little Suha hanging onto the rear fender. Our parents only noticed when the car pulled away, dragging Suha on the ground behind it. Suha was screaming like crazy. Uncle couldn't hear her because of the noise from the engine. We all ran after him, but he only stopped when a man, who had seen us running and shouting frantically, stood in front of the car. Suha was still clinging to the car, screaming and screaming when Papa pried open her grip and lifted her up in his arms. Blood was running from her knees, and her small body was shaking with fear.

"It was her! It was Saada!" she screamed, pointing at me. However, the pampering she got from family and friends, and the presents, erased my feelings of guilt and quieted my conscience.

❧

Once I was invited with my sister to a party. I did my hair in a way I thought looked nice and put on the one silk dress I owned. Should I put on lipstick? Eyeliner? . . . It wouldn't be me. They would know that I was trying to copy them, that I didn't know how to draw the thin line of eyeliner on my eyelid or how to put rouge on my cheeks so that it looked natural. They would laugh at me. I didn't need that. I replaced my feelings of inferiority with an outlook which would restore my self-confidence. I was different: I was natural. Surely there must be boys who preferred the natural look to a girl wearing lots of makeup. Did those little idiot girls imagine that wearing makeup would attract boys, lure them, when actually, it was only they who delighted in it. Their dressing up was just a competition among themselves where they tried to outdo one another.

My sister and I entered the lobby packed with boys and girls. My sister hurried over to her friends, leaving me standing by myself.

"Saada, hi!"

The girl whose party it was greeted me; then she quickly went off to take care of the other guests. The polite welcome. What should I do with myself? I gazed slowly around the lobby. I knew hardly anybody there. But then in the far corner I spotted Sameera, Nuha, and Nabeel. I decided to go and join them. But before I had even moved, two young boys I didn't know went up to them, and they all burst out laughing. What would I do among them? I turned my back on them and started studying intently an oil painting hanging on the wall. Behind me the murmur of conversation and the shouts and laughter gnawed at me, reminding me that I was the odd one out, a stranger, the one who's different because she's natural. I didn't manage to blot out my feelings of inferiority that time. The record player was blaring loudly so I turned to watch the dancers and listen to the singer: "I'm going to buy a paper doll that I can call my own. A doll that other fellows cannot steal . . ."

The singer was just like me: alone, needing the warmth of someone, of . . .

"Saada, would you like to dance?"

I hadn't paid any attention to anyone around me. My heart leapt in my chest, and I felt myself blushing, my face burning. Embarrassment? Bliss? The scent of victory? I placed my hand on Nabeel's shoulder, and he put his arm around my waist. What should I say to him? What should I talk to him about? Thoughts rushed into my head, one after the other. I looked around: all the others were dancing and talking. I didn't know what to say. My anxiety mounted. I was tongue-tied.

The dance ended without either of us uttering a word. Nabeel went back to the corner where his friends were. No one else was polite enough to dance with a fat, ugly girl who, above all else, was stupid and couldn't make conversation. I left quietly and went back home.

2

She heard her come in, so she shut her eyes and pretended to be asleep.

"You didn't eat a thing, Sitt Saada. That just won't do!"

The nurse stroked her hands gently to wake her, then said loudly, "Sitt Saada, Sitt Saada!"

She was obliged to open her eyes. The pale, round face of the nurse leaned over her: "If you don't eat, I'll tell the doctor."

The nurse took a forkful of food from the plate and brought it up to the patient's mouth. *Was she going to refuse it? What was the use?* She opened her mouth slowly, and the nurse popped the food in, watching her chew slowly.

"Doctor Labeeb asked me about you. He'll check on you after ten. I told him your temperature was down yesterday."

She stopped talking, waiting for some reaction. When the patient didn't say anything, she continued, "He suggested we feed you something besides questions. We want you to get your strength back."

The nurse fed her again.

"If I leave you now, do you promise that you'll finish your breakfast by yourself?"

"I'm not hungry," she replied listlessly.

"But you've got to eat!"

"It won't do me any good to eat when I don't feel hungry."

The patient does seem to be getting better. She's talking! She's arguing! I thought she had lost the ability to speak. She's been here for a week, and she hasn't spoken a word to me until now.

"No, it's good for you, even if you eat when you don't feel hungry."

The nurse brought up a third forkful: "Do I have to stay with you, or are you going to eat it on your own?"

No reply. She opened her mouth, then shut her eyes again. The nurse's patience was running out: "Well, what have you decided?"

※

"What have you decided?"

The eternal question, repeated ad infinitum: What have you decided? Have you really thought about it? What did you base your decision on?

Once made, would this decision affect anything? Surely it would never affect history in any way! History! In school we studied the chain of events which filled the void of the distant past and which happened to the people suspended there.

"What's the name of the British general who fought Siraj Dowla in India and took back Calcutta?"

I raised my hand enthusiastically and said, "Robert Clive. Was Calcutta a British city, Miss?"

I can still see the cynical smile on her lips as she replied, "Of course not. However, the British did have commercial interests in India."

"And the Indians?"

"Don't ask questions that get us off the subject, Saada! Now, underline the following in your books."

We opened our books, took out our rulers and pens, and, with heads bowed, drew line after line.

Clive? India? Names and events in the history books. What do they have to do with me? But the words *took back Calcutta*—how can someone take back what isn't his? Do words mean what they mean, and we distort that meaning, or are there two truths contained within the meaning? Several truths, maybe? What's the point of studying history, then? So, I failed the history final.

But what really interested me was language: words, synonyms and antonyms, words with opposite meanings, words whose meaning changed over time, words whose meaning changed through use, words whose meanings were altered through someone's point of view.

It was my mother's dream that I study medicine. Her father was a doctor; her older brother was a doctor. Since she hadn't been blessed with a boy and I was doing well at school, she saw me as the last possible link in the doctor chain. When I was little, I got presents like a stethoscope, a doctor's bag, a hypodermic syringe. Then I got a small microscope. As I got older, books: *The Medicine of the Ancient Egyptians, The History of Arab Medicine, Magic and Medicine.* I read them furiously. I read them because they talked about man's intellect, his beliefs, his imagination. Mama didn't know that I had never read one book in school about the human body, chemistry, or the other sciences which served as a grounding for studying medicine—maybe because the school administration deemed these sciences as uninteresting, unenjoyable, and of no great use to girls. The result was that I got my high school diploma without ever knowing what oxygen, carbonic acid, virility, the collarbone, or the jugular vein were.

"How can I take up medicine when I don't know anything about it?"

"The university can teach you. You can do medicine at the university," Mama replied in all sincerity.

"I'm not interested in medicine," I retorted angrily. "I don't even like science!"

"How can you like or dislike something when you don't know anything about it?"

We got caught up in an circle of pointless questions and answers until my father interrupted, "Let her study what she likes!"

"The point is, should she just study what's fun for her, or something useful?"

I remembered what she had said to her friend: "She can enter some profession so she won't need a husband to support her."

I cried out in defiance, "It's my life. Let me decide for myself!"

She glared at me: "Have you really thought about it? What did you base your decision on?"

⁊

My mother had a number of English friends whom I saw whenever they visited, often to borrow books from my parents' large collection. One time my mother asked me to go to one of their homes for a book they had borrowed several months earlier. My mother told me how to get there. I rang the doorbell. A few minutes later a boy about my age opened the door, so I asked to see "Mrs. Setney." He left me standing at the door and called out "Mummy," then disappeared. A few minutes later, a tall, slender blonde woman appeared—Mrs. Setney.

Two steely blue eyes shot me a cold, inquiring glance, as though asking, "Who are you?"

I introduced myself and asked for my mother's book.

"Wait!"

She shut the door in my face. I hung around outside, waiting—five minutes, ten minutes. Had she forgotten about me? Why did she shut the door in my face? Did she think I was a thief? I felt humiliated and embarrassed. A wave of anger swept over me, but I didn't dare ring the bell again. Let Mama get her own book! As I turned on my heels, the door opened, and the maid held out the book to me. I took it and ran and ran, ran to leave my humiliation behind. Did they treat me like that because I was ugly, dark-skinned, because I wasn't blonde like her, like my friend Kristel? My father sent me to a school for foreigners where most of the students were European. We were very young. We played together. We invited each other to our birthday parties. I never felt there was any difference in appearance between them and me or even a difference in language since I had rapidly picked up the language in which all the subjects were taught. At the end of the school year, the governing body held an open day for our parents and families. We performed a play, sang songs, put on a gymnastics display. My parents didn't understand one word of the play or songs, but they sat there like the other parents, happy to be supportive of their daughters. The open day closed with an awards ceremony for the top students.

At the end of my third school year, we lined up after the gymnastics display and sang the school song. A hush descended as we waited for the awards ceremony. The principal started calling out the names of the prize winners, the youngest first.

"Fritz Schmidt!"

Applause. Fritz left his seat, received his prize, and walked back.

"Rita David!"

Applause. Rita approached the principal, took her books, and returned to her seat.

"Saada Rayyis!"

A ringing in my ears. I must be hallucinating! There was no way I could have done better than my classmates. I'm the Arab girl. Once again, "Saada Rayyis!"

I felt a hand push me from behind. I got up from my row and walked as if in a dream, the ringing and applause sounding in my ears. No, the principal's handshake and the book in my hand were proof that I wasn't dreaming! I returned to my seat.

"Rosemarie Emburger!"

My friend Kristel kissed me. Kristel was sitting by me in the row. We played together in the playground. She told me about how beautiful her own country, Germany, was where she spent her summer vacations. At the end of every vacation, I would wait impatiently for her to get back so we could carry on where we left off. At the beginning of one school year, though, I noticed Kristel with a blonde girl I had never seen before. I ran towards her, holding out my arms to hug Kristel and give her a welcome-back kiss, but she turned her face away as though she didn't recognize me and kept talking to the new girl. I froze on the spot, baffled, dumbstruck. Had I changed so much in one summer that she no longer recognized me?

"Kristel, it's me, Saada!"

She placed her arm through her friend's arm and walked away. Fortunately, I didn't let them see the tears of degradation and humiliation that I could not hold back. Why had Kristel changed? Did she stop liking me because I was ugly, just as my mother had? I would never love anyone again. That way I would never lose anyone.

But as time went by, I started to become aware of something that went beyond me and my ugliness and which robbed me of the last of my childhood innocence. Kristel had changed because she was no longer a child, and Mrs. Setney had humiliated me because she was an adult and I was a child. I knew that my country, Palestine, had a British ruler and Arab subjects, just as India had a British ruler and Indian subjects. Were ruler and subject equal? My maturity helped me forget the pain and insult to my pride Mrs. Setney and Kristel had made me feel, but it could not wipe out the insult to my national pride. My passion grew with the way that this nationalism was expressed, in my language, then by the literature of that language.

ॐ

"What have you decided?"

The same insistent question. She would want to feed me mouthful after mouthful, one after the other, one after the other.

"I can eat it by myself. Thank you, go on back to your work."

A wide smile covered the nurse's face. She patted the patient on the hand: "Well done, now you're acting like an intelligent woman."

The nurse left the room. The patient's eyes darted to the door coming to a gentle close, then to the white walls of the room, and finally came to a rest on a picture hanging opposite her: a print of the Van Gogh painting "Irises in a Jug." The flowers—every shade of blue, from the lightest to the darkest of blues— raised their heads as if proud of their blueness. Why had the artist snapped the stems of two of them? She stared at the irises with the broken stems, their heads bowed down over the wooden table. Was it the balance of the painting he wanted to maintain by contrasting the bright yellow background with the blue irises? Was it to symbolize his defeated spirit, to obliterate the certainty of death? The defeated spirit . . . Death . . .

๛

I was eight years old, and the school bus drivers were on strike, so I couldn't take the bus to school. My parents put me in an orphanage near the school, where I was to stay while the strike lasted. The woman who ran the orphanage was one of my relatives. I was given a room, and a Miss Hikmat was told to look after me. After my parents said good-bye to me, she put my clothes in the closet. Just as she was leaving, she said, "You can go down to the playground until it's time for dinner." I went down. The playground was packed with girls my age and older, all looking at the "new girl." They invited me to play with them. When the dinner bell sounded, I lined up with them, and we all went into an incredibly enormous hall where there were about fifteen or twenty long tables. On each table there were aluminum plates, and on each plate were two slices of brown bread, some olives, and dried figs. I sat with my new playmates on the wooden bench in front of the table, eating happily, surrounded by the hubbub of talk going back and forth, in a situation totally unfamiliar to me.

"Saada, what are you doing here?"

The voice and the hand on my shoulder startled me. I turned round to see Miss Hikmat staring angrily. What had I done?

"I'm having dinner."

"Come with me, right now!"

I felt the blood burning in my face and the tears gathering in my eyes as I said, "I haven't done anything!"

Without reply, she dragged me from the bench. I could feel hundreds of inquisitive eyes staring at me. I lowered my head and walked in silence, while she nudged me along until we got outside.

"What did I do?"

I repeated the question, tears running down my cheeks. She bent down and wiped away the tears.

17

"That's the orphans dining hall. Your papa paid a lot of money for your meals."

She took my hand and led me through the corridor until we came to a door. She opened it, and I followed her into a small dining room with a round table in the middle covered by a white cotton tablecloth, a white china plate, and a silver knife and fork. She sat me down at the table and disappeared, then came back carrying a tray. She placed in front of me a plate with some slices of roast meat, boiled beans, and fried potatoes; a dish of salad; and a bowl containing a piece of *nammoura* and a banana.

"This is *your* dinner, Saada. If you want more, ring the bell."

She left. I sat there alone, eating, wrapped in a heavy silence. For the six months I spent at the orphanage, I never ate anything more mouthwatering and delicious than the olives, brown bread, and dried figs which had been half of my first meal there.

Although they wouldn't let me eat what the other girls ate, they let me play with them. When Mama and Papa visited me after my first week away from home, I introduced them to my new friends, and especially to Najla Saad, my best friend.

"She's the principal's niece!" I stated proudly.

"Badia's daughter?" Papa said. "So, you're related to us. Perhaps, then, you can keep an eye on Saada."

My friendship with Najla grew although she was three years older than I. After I had gone back home, Najla and her mother used to visit us from time to time.

But our relationship had cooled off by the time the child of eight had become a teenager. I was in my final year at school and was getting ready to go to college.

"And what about you, Najla?"

That was the question I posed to her after babbling on about the university I was going to, about getting ready for the journey, about the sort of clothes Mama had in mind for me to wear. I was totally self-absorbed and pleased with myself. Fat, ugly? No, intelligent. The university had accepted me. All my attention was centered on myself, and I thought I was the center of attention for other people as well.

That was the question I posed to her as I was sorting through the books I was going to take with me. When she didn't say anything, I looked up and saw tears running silently down her cheeks. My hand froze on a book, and I asked, "Najla, what's the matter?"

Instead of replying, she ran out of the room, and I heard the front door slam. What was wrong with her? A few minutes later, my mother came into the room wanting to know what had happened, so I told her. She gave me an angry stare: "Don't you care about other people's feelings?"

She saw the look of amazement and incomprehension on my face and said, "Have you forgotten Najla doesn't have a father, that she has to work for a living, that she can't go and study at college? How can you insult her like that?"

The embarrassment burned in my face, but so did the anger of being unjustly accused.

"I didn't insult her! I never meant to!"

My mother had accused me of insulting Najla, and she was the one who had forbidden me to make friends with Afaf because her father was a laundryman! Should I have told her that? Should I have accused her of double standards? I was going away soon, thank God, and would be rid of her. So I kept silent.

Before I set off for Cairo, Najla went to Libya to work in a hospital. Two years later, we heard she had been killed in a car crash . . . The defeated spirit . . . Death.

◈

They met once a week—the European professors appointed by their countries to work in several of the Beirut institutes. They met to read European literature—poetry and prose, novels, meditations —and then discuss the readings for content, style, and meaning.

They had just finished discussing Goethe's *The Sorrows of Young Werther*, so I asked one of them, "What should we read for next time?"

"How about some poetry for a change?"

"We spent all of last year reading poetry. No, another novel."

"Another German novel?"

Suddenly, the leader of the discussion group looked at me.

"We've been in this country for years, and we still don't know a thing about Arabic literature."

All turned their eyes to me.

"Why don't we take advantage of Saada's presence here among us and get her to introduce us to some modern Arabic literature?"

"Great!"

"A terrific idea!"

The group leader asked me, "Can you translate into other languages?"

"There are some poems and novels which have already been translated in the library."

"So, we're agreed. Choose whatever you deem suitable, and we'll spend the rest of the year getting acquainted with Arabic literature."

I went down to the library, feelings of pride welling in me: foreigners were actually interested in Arabic literature, willing to study it even in translation. This was a chance for me to show them the splendors of our literature, its variety and artistry, and a chance to restore to the "subject" the respect of the "ruler." And what of the "subject"—my fellow countryman? I smiled to myself. He wasn't interested in literature, wasn't even aware of its existence! I felt a contempt of another kind as I flipped through the books on the shelves, poring over the translations. In the end, I got out some contemporary Arabic poetry, a play, *The Sultan's Dilemma,* by Tewfiq Hakeem, and a novel, *Season of Migration to the North,* by Tayyeb Salih.

"What shall we start with?"

"With the play. If we like it, we'll still have enough time to learn the lines and perform it at the end of the year."

My pride swelled when I saw how enthusiastic they were at the prospect of reading and discussing the play and how they were bound to admire its originality, symbolism, and meaning.

"We're going to perform it then?"

"Yes."

They assigned the roles so they could learn them. I moved onto poetry, starting with "Hymn to the Rain," which I thought was one of Sayyab's most beautiful poems. One of them finished reading it with a loud "Hmmm." I looked up from my book to a lot of stares. Where was the admiration I had expected? I scrutinized their faces only to see the signs of disappointment. I started to blush.

"Didn't you like it?"

No one answered, so I said sharply, "It's one of the most beautiful poems in our modern poetry!"

The group leader then said, "Actually, Saada, it just shows the difficulty of translating poetry."

It was true, the rhythm of Arabic poetry couldn't be translated. I was trying to give them an idea of this rhythm, and I had failed miserably again. The European ear is used to heavy and light stress in the rhythm of its poetry, so how could that ear appreciate what is more delicate and subtle, say in the difference between voweled and unvoweled letters in the stress patterns of Arabic words?

Conceited Europeans! Even I laughed when I saw their smiles as they studied the translated images. In fact, the image loses its poetry entirely when it is translated into another language. The imagination, too, is linked to a certain environment, heritage, and culture.

"Let's move onto the prose. I think you'll enjoy *Season of Migration to the North* as much as Hakeem's play."

This was my second surprise.

"We've read and understood it. No music or poetic images there. So why is he so famous?"

Dumbfounded, I listened to their views.

"I don't understand why Mustafa Saeed killed all those women."

"Neither did I. I felt the novel was a story of a crime without a motive."

"Yes, especially since Tayyeb Saleh portrays the protagonist as an educated and cultured man, a graduate of one of England's best universities."

"Really, we felt his actions were most unconvincing."

I listened and listened. Then the startling truth dawned on me: *Ruler and Subject!* And I laughed. I laughed until the tears ran down my cheeks, but I got a hold of myself when I saw them staring strangely at me. The tears still streaming, I said, "East is East and West is West, and never the twain shall meet!"

One of them looked clearly annoyed and said, "What's Kipling got to do with it?"

I was afraid they'd think I was being sarcastic so I hurriedly explained, "My friends, you read the novel from the perspective of a people who have not only ruled themselves, but ruled others, whereas we read it from the perspective of a people who have never ruled themselves."

I began to explain what Tayyeb Saleh was trying to say to make them realize that Mustafa Saeed's resentment and his revenge only represented the pain and hope of an oppressed people.

"Wasn't that one of the most enjoyable readings we've had?" one of the group said after the discussions and explications had concluded. Laughing, I asked, "Now don't you agree this is a great novel?"

They were silent for a while, then somebody said, "Yes, but, we find you somewhat curious."

"Me?"

I was speechless.

"Yes, you. Your western education and Arab roots. You speak our language as well as we do, behave like we do, like what we like, share our tastes, so how can you see something we cannot?"

It all came back to me: the history lesson about Clive of India, the image of Kristel and Mrs. Setney, the pain of humiliation and degradation that not even the long years had been able to wipe out, and the hatred I had buried deep inside because the weak have no other recourse but to bury their hatred.

"Because I'm not one of you."

3

She ate the last forkful of food, pushed the table away from her bed, then turned her face toward the window: wispy clouds swam in the blue autumn skies, and just outside the window bare branches tossed, stirred by the breeze. Her eyes followed the movement of the branches for a little while, then went back to watching the clouds as they joined to form a sheep. Its tail grew longer and longer, obscuring the infinite blue, becoming a gray, solid mass. She concentrated on its density . . . How much longer was the doctor going to keep her here?

She gazed back around the room, her eyes falling on a bouquet of white carnations on a table in the corner. Why hadn't she noticed it before? Sumayya, her students, weren't they missing her? She reached out and pressed the bell. A few minutes later, the nurse's head peered around the door.

"Yes?"

"I've finished my breakfast, Miss."

"Wonderful, the doctor will be pleased."

She came in, picked up the tray, and pushed the table back into its corner.

"Who're these carnations from?" she asked, pointing to them. "I was asleep when they came yesterday evening. There's a card in them."

Carrying the tray in one hand, the nurse went up and picked out a small envelope stuck among the flowers. She read out the name on the envelope as she held it out to the patient.

"Miss Saada Rayyis. Do you need anything else?"

"Nothing, thank you."

She waited until the nurse had closed the door behind her, then carefully opened the envelope and pulled out a small card. She stared at the name. What? Her hand began to shake. How did he know I was here? He had even remembered what her favorite flowers were! Twenty-two years! And of course, there was nothing on it except his name.

పొ

"Egyptian?"

"No, Palestinian."

"But you look Egyptian and you have an Egyptian accent. I'm from Lebanon, Ali Saber."

"I can tell from your accent. My mother was Lebanese. My name's Saada Rayyis."

"Are you a student here?"

"Faculty of arts, department of Arabic. What about you?"

"Faculty of engineering, department of architecture."

After that I only ran into him by accident. Saada the monkey? No, the chameleon. Why did the thought of a chameleon disgust me when I was one? In Jerusalem I had a Palestinian accent. I had only spent three months in Cairo and already I had an Egyptian accent. No, my accent was my own.

"Are you Syrian? You look and talk like an Egyptian."

"No, I'm Palestinian."

"That's Syrian?"

"Syria is in Syria."

"But look, you're all Syrians, easterners."

How can Syria be in Palestine? Just because Egypt is west of Palestine, does that make me an easterner? To me a westerner is a European, an American. Does "The West" to Egyptians mean something other than what it does in my native dialect? Language, once again. I was majoring in language and literature then. In Ibn Khaldoun's *Mulladina,* I was stunned by one section which read "Wherever the Arabs conquer, destruction follows in their wake." Unbelievable! I also read "The epitome of their way of life is characterized by nomadism and conquest." So, he means the desert Arabs, the Bedouin. The epithet "Arab" meant one thing to Ibn Khaldoun and something else to me, just as "Syrian" and "easterner" to Egyptians meant something different to me. My passion for linguistics grew as did my passion for Egypt and Egyptians.

Since nobody at the university knew my mother or sister, no one could compare me to them. Dark-skinned? The Egyptian women were dark-skinned. Fat? No one disapproved of obesity in Egypt. Here I was just considered "not like everyone else" or "different." I attracted attention, I stirred up curiosity. I also made friends. For the first time in my life I made friends and felt that I belonged. I acted in *Othello;* I attended lectures by Tewfiq Hakeem, Lutfi Sayyid, Taha Hussein. If language determined my ethnic grouping, the way I spoke showed that I belonged to the group of young men and women with whom I regularly traveled to Helwaan. Or so I thought. I spoke as they spoke. I told the same jokes, shared the same interests and concerns—interests expressed by their jokes, concerns expressed by their demonstrations.

I had never seen, nor taken part in a demonstration before I came to Cairo. Maybe it was because I was so young, so unaware, so sheltered. But when Bahaa and Anis told me about the student demonstration, which was to set off from the university, in protest against the president's tyranny, I agreed to join it without hesitation. I didn't sleep at all that night. Maybe I was so nervous because, for the very first time, I was taking part in a political movement. Maybe I was just happy we were able to voice our opinions and effect change. Anyway, this is what I thought. Early the following morning, we gathered in the university precinct. I had never seen so many students in my life. I felt really proud: I was one of them, and together we were going to force the president to change his policies or resign. When the wave of students began to pour through the gate of the main courtyard, their shouts getting louder and louder, I concentrated all my strength in my throat, erasing the physical, sexual, and cultural differences between me and them. I wasn't Saada—my own individuality was lost, dissolved in that awe-inspiring and tumultuous sea. I repeated the slogans without thinking, moved along without thinking, knew nothing but the fanaticism that grew stronger and stronger and the fire in my voice, our voice. But then, shots, followed by more shots, and a shout rose up, a shout of a different kind. The ranks in front of us crumbled, and the students started running in all directions, and I along with them. I ran without thinking, pursued by screams and gunfire. I ran and ran until I could hear nothing more and found myself with some other students in a empty alley. Only later that afternoon did we learn that the soldiers had waited for the vanguard of the demonstration to cross the bridge; then they had surrounded it from the front and rear, cutting it off from the bulk of the demonstrators, before attacking the students with a hail of whips, rifle butts, and bullets. The administration didn't fall, and neither did the president change his policies. I and my fellows wept over the four students who had been killed. I didn't know who they were, nor to which college they belonged, but I never felt they were any different from me. This alienation had become for me a sense of belonging, and the differences similarities. I felt the word to mean the thing itself and its opposite. The chameleon had changed color.

৵

"Saada, how you've changed!"

Their looks of surprise and disbelief were my revenge on them when I came back to Jerusalem for the summer vacation after the first school year—a well-dressed, self-confident woman who would return any smart remark with twice the sting. My shyness had disappeared but not my feelings of inferiority. I was greeted by the faces of my mother and my sister every day. Suha, as usual, got invited to parties, received phone calls, was visited by friends. And my own friends? Well, they were all in Cairo.

"Saada, you're home safe, thanks be to God. When are you going back? How's Cairo? How's college?"

Then they would turn back to Suha and pick up their conversation where they left off, not even waiting for me to reply. Was it because Egypt didn't interest them, because I didn't interest them? They must have felt inferior, jealous because I was a student at a university they had never dreamed of getting into and because I was more intelligent and more knowledgeable. I imagined they were jealous since I was better than them. It was only years later that I realized it was my superior attitude and knowing airs which drove them away. But then I thought it was feelings of inferiority and envy on their part, when all along it was nothing more than lack of interest. So why should what I was studying interest them, or the language and its literature? Should life necessarily be a subject and topic of study? If one of them had told me about something in particular, I would not have listened with any greater interest than they listened to me, or with greater respect for that matter. But none of this occurred to a student who considered knowledge everything in life, and who had erected around herself a wall of self-importance and indifference.

That first vacation, my uncle who had gone to live in Brazil before I was born came to visit. Mama was proud of her younger brother, and she was always going on about his self-made success and the great wealth that he had amassed through hard work and intelligence. When his wife died, Mama opened our house to receive the mourners.

"But Mama, you didn't even know her!"

"She was my sister-in-law. She was so young. How can I not feel sad for her, or for my brother?"

Whenever she got a letter from him, she would read it out to us so we would get to hear about the new store he had opened, the large villa he had moved to, the modern furniture he had imported from Italy. Fortunately, there weren't many letters. So when we received a telegram telling us that he and his daughter were coming, Suha and I got to guessing what sort of presents he was going to give us.

"Brazil is famous for its precious stones. I'm sure he's going to give us all jewelry!"

"All you think about is jewelry!" I teased Suha.

But I was dreaming of expensive presents as well. The long-awaited day finally came. Mama put flowers all around the house, and we put on our best dresses. When we heard a car stopping in front of the garden gate, Suha and I ran out to welcome the bearer of all this fabled treasure. He got out of the car. He was tall and slender. He had Mama's green eyes and her beautiful features. Loretta got out behind him. I stopped in my tracks—I had never before in my life seen a young woman as beautiful and elegant. She was as tall and slender as her father, and in her olive-colored face, two large brown eyes sparkled as if she had applied eyeliner around them, or maybe it was just her long black eyelashes. The strange thing was, though, she had an olive complexion but hair that shone like gold.

"Saada, don't you want to meet your cousin?"

I went up to her, but I was afraid of messing up or getting her white, silk suit dirty, so I planted a kiss on her cheek without touching her body. However, she clasped her long arms around me and drew me to her.

"Aren't you Saada, the smart one?"

I fell in love with her foreign accent and the dimples that appeared in her cheeks when she smiled.

The presents didn't appear that day, nor the next. It became quite clear to Suha and me that there weren't going to be any presents.

"Maybe they don't usually give gifts in Brazil."

"He might be buying the presents here."

"That's got to be it. But how does he know what we want?"

Then we both forgot the subject as the days passed, and he never bothered to give us anything.

One day, I came back from the souk all excited.

"Mama, you won't believe it! I found Mutannabi's *Diwan* in the souk, the one with Akbari's commentary!"

When my enthusiasm was met with an odd look, I added, "It's a rare book, so it's expensive."

Wasn't a rich uncle supposed to be generous?

"How much is it?" he actually asked.

"Ten pounds." I tried to look and sound as winsome as possible.

"I'll buy it for you tomorrow."

Mama then cut in tersely: "No. I just can't allow it."

The harshness in her voice reduced me to silence, sending to flight any dream of Akbari. It was pure spite: Mama was denying me the book because it was just for me and not for Suha as well. She was, as usual, being hateful towards me. I didn't realize that Mama was refusing his gift because she knew what a skinflint he was. Rather than letting him buy me the book as a gift, she preferred to keep him indebted to her hospitality so that her honor would not be diminished by his riches. I held back the tears of anger and indignation. Of course, my uncle never did buy me the book.

Before he returned to Brazil, Mama took him around to say good-bye to some friends. Loretta was asleep. When they came back at eleven, the door to Loretta's room was still closed.

"Hasn't your cousin had breakfast?"

Cousin, not *Loretta.* Mama must have been angry.

"She's still asleep."

I then got the full weight of her reprimand: "You mean you haven't served her any breakfast? Have you forgotten that you're her host? You selfish girl, don't you think about anyone but yourself?"

This time, though, my temper boiled over and I screamed, "Should I wake her up if she's asleep? If she's hungry, she can get up!"

I didn't dare add, "I'm not her servant. Does anyone serve me breakfast in bed?" I stormed off to my room and slammed the door shut. Alone, and rejected! They hate me! I never realized that my uncle might just be stingy. His selfishness, the extra work his stay had meant for us, the additional expense, Papa's embarrassment—all this had strained Mama's nerves, and I was the scapegoat. This never crossed my mind while I considered myself the center of the universe.

So, I announced my intention to go back to Egypt.

"But college doesn't start for a month!"

"I can stay at my aunt's. All my friends are there," I insisted.

"Don't you like your home or family any more?" Mama's green eyes emitted sparks of fury, or was it injured pride, or maybe she felt she was being rejected as a mother.

"I like Egypt better."

"You rude, ungrateful child!"

"You should be happy then that you're getting rid of me, since I'm so rude and ungrateful. Don't worry, dear sweet Suha will be here for you."

I went to my room, closed the door on them, and got back to my books. When would I be rid of them and be independent again? When could I live alone, go out on my own, make decisions on my own, be with those I liked and who liked me? The gulf between me and my family was growing wider. "A stranger in my own family, more at home with strangers," I thought during that first summer. Not until years later did I grasp Tarafa's saying, "One you did not provide for nor expected to hear from will bring news." At that time I kept asking myself, "What does it mean to belong? Is it like wearing a dress and then putting on another a month or a year later?"

♣

He was in the same class. Was he Turkish, Syrian? Anyway, Amer told me he was Egyptian. But he had gray eyes, a fine, straight nose, and small mouth. He was handsome. There was nothing Egyptian about him except his accent and his charm. Even his clothes were smarter than the ones the other students wore.

"Do you know French?"

Those were the first words he spoke to me, even though he had been in my class for two years. He wanted my help in reading Massignon's book on Hallaj. Now I was thankful for the trouble Mama had taken over my appearance before I came to the university—I wore a different dress whenever I saw Amer in an effort to keep up with his trendy style.

"Are you going to pay me back for Massignon?" I said to him, half-joking, but before he could reply, I added, "I need you, Amer, to explicate the Quran."

We met every day, even after we had finished Hallaj and the sura of "The Bee." Or was Hallaj and the sura just an excuse? I was no longer thinking about whether I was fat or ugly. In fact, for the first time, I was thinking about what dress to wear and whether the blouse would go with the skirt, whether to put on eyeliner or lipstick, whether I would look good for that handsome young man who had chosen me, in spite of myself, from among my friends, because I was "not like everyone else, different." Maybe it was because I spoke French. But none of those questions came to mind while I was seeing a young man who was interested in me as a person. For the first time in my life, after years of deprivation my young blood was stirring. I was in love. I forgot that the one who never loves will never experience conflict nor the loss of the one she loves. I was in love, and I guarded my love behind a wall of secrecy. I was like others, like Naeema who, I discovered, was in love with Saad and met with him in secret, except for the time she was sick and asked me to meet him behind the library to apologize for her absence. She asked me because I was "not like everyone else" and she thought me "different" and because I was from a place where people didn't disapprove of young men and women seeing each other, who didn't consider love a sin that had to be hidden.

During lectures, I sat in the front row while Amer sat in the back. Between lectures, everyone gathered with classmates of the same sex, neither looking at nor talking with the other. But as soon as the lectures were over, I rushed to meet him at the zoo or Uzbekiyya Park or Casino Biba. From there, we often headed to the cinema, not to watch the movie, but just to hold hands in the dark. He would squeeze my hand and press his leg up against mine, which sent the blood pulsing through my veins and made my heart pound. I neither watched the screen nor listened to what the actors were saying. All I heard was his heavy breathing right by my ear, while I felt the sweat from his hand moistening my own feverish palm.

On Friday, our day off, I would say to Atayet, my dorm roommate, "I'm off to the Dar al-Kutub bookstore. They have a lot of old books on Islamic philosophy."

"What about the university library—isn't it good enough for you?"

I made a quick exit so my smile didn't give me away. I met him at the station since we were going to spend the day at Maadi Park or Helwaan. We always chose a remote, secluded spot where we could lie on the grass, my head on his shoulder, or his head on mine, or cheek to cheek. It didn't take long before our lips were pressed together in a long, hungry, passionate kiss, while existence dissolved around us. At the end of the day, I returned to the student dorm.

"Are you through reading?"

I replied to Atayet, a wicked smile on my face, "Through? Is mankind ever through?"

I lay back on my bed and closed my eyes.

At that time, all I kept up of my former habits was going to church once a week. On Sunday, I would get up early to go pray before the eight o'clock lecture. I forgot my homesickness, my feeling that I was different as I repeated along with the others the prayers and chants I had known since I was little. Did I realize that what I thought I had rejected was, in fact, drawing and tying me to it so that I wouldn't feel homesick or loss. I don't know. I believed that turning to religion was my own decision, a decision free from any outside influence. It was as if reaching this decision on my own confirmed my complete separation from my family—that is, until something happened which showed me my faith was only another facet of the strong bond that tied me to them.

٭

"Saada, I've got a letter for you from Doctor Taha."

"Doctor Taha? Who's he?"

"Don't you remember? You were with me in his office last week when I handed in my research paper. He was asking you about your country and your family."

"Oh yes! But what does he want?"

"It seems he likes you."

Atayet handed me a sealed envelope. He likes me? But we only met the once! I opened the letter.

He had to be crazy! A marriage proposal! He was going to write to my parents. I reread it. I couldn't believe it. What was Papa going to think when he got a letter from this man? My heart started to pound. No way! I had to write to my parents right away so they wouldn't think I was being rash and irresponsible. *My father used to wait for me on the balcony whenever I went out. I would see him as soon as I walked around the bend where the road began. When he saw me coming, he would get out his pocket watch, which was attached by a golden chain to his jacket buttonhole, glance quickly at it, then say dryly, "Half-past six, Saada!"*

He would scold me because I was half an hour later than expected, a half-hour later than allowed.

But what about Amer? That wasn't being rash or irresponsible. It was love.

"What does the letter say?" I heard Atayet ask as if from another world. I remained silent. I was embarrassed for him. Here was a professor of long standing, a doctor of economics, proposing marriage to a young woman he didn't even know, not even his own age, nationality, or religion, the one who was "not like everyone else, different." But what about Amer?

"Well?"

My face was bright red. If he wasn't embarrassed, why was I? I handed the letter to her.

"Oh, you're so lucky!"

"Me, lucky?"

I was speechless with astonishment.

"I wish a university professor would ask me to marry him!"

She was judging me by her standards, thinking her values were my values, her way of thinking was mine. I replied angrily, "Here, you take it then. I'll only marry someone I love!"

❧

We were in the study break before the final examinations. There was a light knock on my door.

"Saada, telephone."

Who could it be, Amer? I was only with him yesterday. He was studying, like me. My Aunt Asma, maybe? She knew I was studying for the exams. I wondered, What does she want? I hurried down the stairs.

"Hello?"

"Saada Rayyis?" I heard a man's voice say.

"Yes."

"My name's Hasan Damanhouri. I work in the Red Crescent, and I'm a friend of Doctor Taha's."

Not again. Was he using others, strangers, to call on his behalf? Should I hang up? Didn't he understand that I had refused him?

"I was telling him about a young girl in the refugee camp who had come to my attention and . . ."

I had no idea what he was talking about so I interrupted him: "Refugee camp?"

"Yes, in Sinai. I asked her her name. Suha Rayyis."

I was at a loss for words. My mind was a jumble. Who was he talking about? Suha, my sister Suha? But she was with my parents in Jerusalem.

"I was talking with Doctor Taha about her, since she said she had a sister in Cairo, so he said she might be related to you."

I screamed into the telephone, "My sister? My sister, Suha? How did she end up in a refugee camp in Sinai?"

"She told me she was coming to Cairo to take the British matriculation examinations because the schools in Palestine were closed, and all official examinations had been canceled because of the war. However, our government has denied Palestinians entry to Egypt and has put them up in camps until they return to their country."

"But my sister's not a refugee!"

"More importantly, Miss, she's alone. Quite frankly, I'm afraid for her. I have sisters her age."

"What should I do?" I felt confused, helpless, and desperate.

He answered, "The solution is in the hands of the minister of war. Only the minister can order someone to be taken out of the camp."

How could I get to see the minister, the most important minister in a wartime situation like this? I heard him say, "You're quite fortunate. Doctor Taha is related to his wife. Ask him to speak to the minister."

My mouth went dry. All I could utter was, "Thank you."

But I didn't want him to notice the dryness of my tone, so I repeated with enthusiasm, "I thank you for your generosity, Hasan, Afandi. I really can't thank you enough."

I hung up the phone and just stood there frozen. Speak to him? After what happened? Impossible! The scene replayed itself: a young female student up before a respected professor. He stood up when I entered his office. He wanted me to come closer, but I stayed just inside the threshold, leaving the door open behind me. I blurted out, "I thank you, professor, for placing so much confidence in me and for liking me, but I cannot possibly accept you proposal. I don't know you, and I . . ."

"But we have ample opportunity to get to know each other."

I had rehearsed very word I was going to say to him so I wouldn't injure his pride, but the leer on his face made me forget everything. I suddenly blurted out, "There's a proverb in my country which says, 'The content is clear from its title,' and I have read the title."

I turned and rushed out, closing the door behind me.

Was fate toying with me? I never thought that Doctor Taha would turn up in my life again or that my sister's destiny would be in his hands. Would he get back at me? Would he get to his cousin's husband before me and block my attempt to help my sister. If I had known what fate had in store for me, I would never have acted in the way I did. But we think about fate only after something unexpected or startling happens to us. Then we say, "It's fate—it was meant to be." To think, my sister Suha, beautiful Suha, alone among strangers. Villagers, ruffians maybe? I went back to my room.

"What's the matter?"

I could see my fear reflected in Atayet's eyes as she looked at me.

"My sister's in a refugee camp in Sinai. I've got to get her out of there."

I told her the story. I didn't mention Doctor Taha.

"There's no way you'll get to see the minister of war, Saada, especially just by yourself."

I closed the books and lecture notes that I was studying and sat at my desk where I started writing out my request to the minister. The following morning, I rode the tram to the Ministry of War.

"Yes, Miss?"

The guard stopped me at the outer entrance. My heart began to race, but the image of my sister in the camp formed in my mind. I said in a confident manner, "I need to see the minister."

"Do you have an appointment?"

I ignored the question, looked at my wristwatch, then said in a calm voice, "I know that he's not here yet, but I'll wait, thank you."

I passed through the entrance, stepping purposefully as if I knew that I had a meeting with him. The soldier didn't try to stop me. But where was the minister's office? I didn't dare hesitate in case the guard got suspicious, so I climbed the stairs to the second floor, where a man showed me to the minister's office. I went in, and found myself in a large reception room in which four men were sitting. The secretary sat behind a desk in the left-hand corner. He shot me an inquiring look, so I walked up to him.

"I would like to see the minister."

"Do you have an appointment?"

He then looked at the appointments book in front of him. I wasn't going to get away with it this time. But Suha?

"I wasn't able to get an appointment. A very urgent matter has suddenly arisen, and it's very important that I speak to him personally. Please, I have to see him!"

Was it the urgency in my voice, the imploring look in my eye, my young age, or the fact that I was a girl, because he hesitated for a second, then asked, "Your name, please?"

I felt that my heart was about to burst through my chest when he wrote my name down and said to me, "Please, take a seat."

I sat down. Did the minister have any daughters? How could I persuade him? Had Doctor Taha spoken to him? What was I going to say to him? Then three men and a woman entered the waiting room. The woman was elegant, dressed in a dark blue summer suit. My gaze was drawn to a rose pinned in her hat. They spoke to the secretary for a moment, then took their places to wait just like me. If Amer had had a telephone I would have called him to get his advice. Amer!

I found myself thinking distractedly about our last date. Oh sure, life was sweet. Suha was in a camp! That was . . .

The sound of footsteps in the corridor outside brought me back to the waiting room. The secretary rose to his feet and bowed, hand on chest, as a tall, overweight, well-dressed man in his fifties or sixties entered the room followed by two soldiers and a man carrying a briefcase. The minister! We all stood up. Without looking at us, the minister and his retinue walked straight over to an adjacent room and closed the door behind them. My eye was glued to that door. A few minutes later, when the telephone on the secretary's desk rang, everyone's eyes turned toward him, waiting for him to speak.

"Yes, Afandi."

He replaced the receiver then called out, "Muhammad Afandi, Muhammad Abdul Aziz!"

Two of the men who had been waiting got up and went into the minister's office. So, two more to go before me. I looked at my watch, then went back to my worries. Could I actually persuade the minister, gain his sympathy? But how? I went over what I was going to say and argue for the twentieth time. The door opened and the two men came out. When the next man went in, I could no longer think about anything. I just stared at the door. All I could hear was my heart pounding in my ears. My mind was a blank.

Finally, my turn came. No sooner was the man ahead of me out of the minister's office than I got to my feet and hurried toward the door.

"Just one moment, Miss, you can't go in yet."

I stopped in my tracks. My cheeks felt as though they were on fire. I stood there for a moment, then returned to my seat. I didn't dare raise my head. I was certain everyone was staring at me. I just sat there, examining the design on the floor tiles. The telephone rang. I stole a glance at the secretary from the corner of my eye.

"Miss Saada Rayyis."

I rose, rushed over to the minister's office, and knocked gently on the door.

"Come in."

I went in, quietly closing the door behind me. The minister was sitting behind his desk. To his left was a young man presenting him with some papers to sign. The young man looked up at me, but the minister didn't raise his head until the young man had picked up the last document from in front of him.

"Yes?"

I noticed a look of surprise on his face. Was it because I was only a young woman. I handed over my request without uttering a word. While he read it, I looked hard at his expression, but it didn't give away anything going on in his mind. Of course not, he was a minister, after all! He then raised his head from the paper to me. Silence seemed to reign for an eternity between us. At last I blurted out, "I beg you, Your Excellency, please don't refuse my request!"

I choked on the final word, and every last word and argument I had practiced in my mind flew from my mind. He cleared his throat, then said, "You know full well that I can't allow any Palestinian refugee into Egypt. Their place is in their own country, or the Zionists will take over."

Was there a sympathetic tone in his voice, or was it merely wishful thinking on my part?

"But my sister isn't a refugee! My parents live in Jerusalem, and she'll go back there just as soon as she's finished her exams!"

(It was the second time that fate had made a fool of me in the space of two weeks. Again, I could only tell that it was fate after what happened had happened. Suha couldn't go back to our parents, and I couldn't go back to Jerusalem).

Another eternity of silence followed.

"She's all alone, Your Excellency. I don't know if she's got anything to eat or even if she's got any money!"

I fell silent. Eventually, he replied, "Since she's not a refugee, I'll allow her to leave the camp."

He then bent over my request and wrote a sentence on it, while at the same time ringing a bell on his desk with his other hand. Was the dry tone in his voice to dissuade me from making any other requests. What else was there to ask for on top of my sister's release? When the young man came back in, he handed him my request.

"See to this right away."

My heart danced.

"Thank you, Your Excellency. Thank you!" And crying with joy, I said, "May God protect your children."

I don't remember leaving his office or even taking the tram back to the dorm. I didn't realize the rush I was in until Atayet asked me, "How is Suha going to get to Cairo from Sinai?"

Yes, how was she going to get here? How would I find her? When? My joy flew out the window.

When I met Amer the next day, he quieted my fears.

"Don't worry," he said. "I'm sure the Red Crescent will take care of all that. Wasn't it one of their employees who told you about Suha? She's got your address and phone number."

As usual, Amer put me at ease, made me feel happy, but I felt something was worrying him, something was different.

"What's the matter?"

"Me? Nothing."

We strolled together along the bank of the Nile. Suddenly, he stopped.

"I'm tired of walking, Saada."

"Well, let's go and sit in Casino Biba, then."

"No, come with me to my house."

I froze. His house? He had never invited me before. It suddenly occurred to me that I had been going out with him for a year, and I didn't know anything about his private life. Did he live with his family? On his own? So I asked, my heart trembling with anticipation, "Are you going to introduce me to your family?"

He would now get to know my sister; he wanted to strengthen our family ties. He was thinking about what went beyond love, what love led to.

Without replying, he started to cross the road to the sidewalk opposite, so I grabbed his arm and repeated the question, this time with a little more caution: "You do want to introduce me to your family, Amer?"

He patted my hand and said tenderly, "Isn't it enough that you know me?"

He dragged me along. Why was he acting like this now? To take advantage of me before Suha came? *Take advantage?* Why this phrase? Is this what love was? Suddenly a notion flashed into my mind that terrified me—what if it's not love! Maybe it was just an opportunity to enjoy the company of a girl who was "different," to hug and kiss a girl, and now . . . I stopped walking and stood still.

"Amer, I can't go with you if there's no one at your house."

I was surprised by the fire in his voice and the sparks of anger in his eyes when he replied, "Was there anyone with me in Maadi or Helwaan?" Then he added in a scornful tone, "Or are you only now worried for your reputation because your sister's coming here?"

He grabbed my arm again and started dragging me along, so I just planted my feet and stood firm. Was this the Amer I loved?

"What's the matter with you? Come on, let's walk!"

Walk? No, I didn't think so! I pushed him roughly away from me into the road and took off, running in the direction of the student dorm. Why me? Because I was "different"? Did he think I was easy since Egyptian, Muslim girls didn't let him kiss them? Or did they just kiss in secret? And Naeema's relationship with Saad—was it love or sex? The words "love" and "sex" jostled in my mind as I ran on, panting. Was he coming after me? Could I really say that I was happy being independent, that at last I was living on my own, solving my own problems, making my own decisions? But I had made a decision, and now I was running scared as a result. Only after several minutes had passed did I dare look behind me. I didn't see him. I felt less frightened and went on my way more slowly. What had happened with him? Perhaps I was just easily fooled, blind. A romantic can believe in love, love without sex. But our embraces, our kisses—their memory stirred my sexual desire. I had to admit that I had felt and was feeling sexual desire, but I was in love. And him? Was it both desire and love or just desire? Was I the only one who was actually in love? If he loved me, he would only want to prove it by marrying me. Well, this is what my naiveté and upbringing made me think. I had escaped from an abyss, an abyss into which my heart and my imagination had fallen. Now, Amer appeared to me as a male just out to satisfy his desires, as a man of experience who knew how to slowly seduce a gullible "foreigner." Didn't we share the same values? Didn't we think alike? I remembered I had posed myself the exact same questions a year ago. I smiled bitterly. At that time, I thought it was only Atayet and Doctor Taha who didn't share my way of thinking. Doctor Taha had proposed to me, and I had turned him down. And now?

"Watch out, Miss!"

A cyclist passed by me, barely an inch away, so I screamed at him, "The sidewalk is for pedestrians, not for cyclists!" But all he did was laugh as he cycled away. How deluded I was to think that their values and their way of thinking was closer to mine than the values I was brought up with and the way of thinking based on them. I thought of myself as one of them because I was estranged from my family. I laughed at my stupidity—did I really know "here"? Did I really fit in "here"? The chameleon, after all, can change only its color.

⁂

"But she's my only sister, my little sister!"

"I'm sorry, Saada, but we can only accept university students here."

I pleaded with the dean. I tried to win her sympathy, but it was useless. I would have to look for a place that would take in both my sister and me.

"Be careful, Saada, just remember you're two girls on your own. Make sure that the place has a good reputation before you move in."

I was tempted to tell the dean she didn't practice what she preached, but I kept quiet.

I thought about staying at my aunt's house, but it was too small and too far from the university. We could stay at the YWCA, but my budget wouldn't stretch to that. Finally, I hit upon a charitable housing trust for low-income female employees and factory workers. My heart pounding, I rang the bell, doubting that they would accept us since we were neither. No one answered. I waited a couple of minutes, then tried again. At last, I heard slow, heavy footsteps; then the door opened.

"Can't you wait a minute?"

My eyes froze on a mountain of flesh blocking the doorway. I had never in my life seen a woman her size. She was extremely tall and just as wide, all covered by a red dress with tiny blue flowers. My gaze climbed that red mountain until it met two angry eyes, and I immediately looked down.

"What do you want?"

If she turned me down, my sister and I would be out on the street. This place was my last hope. So with my head still bowed, I gathered my courage and replied as politely and amiably as possible, "A room, a room for my younger sister and me."

The mountain moved to give me room and said dryly, "Please, come in."

I went in. She asked me, "Who sent you to us? Your name? Age? What do you do? Your family?"

I answered all her questions politely and graciously. All the while I was talking, I was asking myself what I was going to do if she turned me down. Where would I go? Then she asked, "How many months do you want the room for?"

Was she going to accept us, depending on how long or short a time I wanted the room for? I didn't know. My heart raced as I answered candidly, "Only three months. Just until my sister has taken her exams."

I searched her face. A mask. After what seemed like an hour, she said, "Fine. We have a room available. You can move in right away."

❧

Three days later, Suha turned up, and I left the dorm to live with her in the charitable trust housing. It was not the beautiful, slim Suha that I envied and hated, but Suha my sister.

ॐ

Suha was busy preparing for her exams, while I was working on research papers I had to hand in before I could start studying for my exams. Every afternoon, when I came back from the university, I would sit opposite Suha at a small table by the window where we would bury our heads in our books and notes. After writing a paragraph or two, I would look up to think, and my gaze would fall on the inclined head in front of me. Feelings of comfort and peace would flow through me; then my mind would wander, far far away from the couplets of Ibn Malek.

"Are you having trouble understanding it?"

Suha's question brought me back, not to the works of Ibn Malek, but to her.

"Not at all, I was just thinking."

"About your studies?"

Should I tell her? I looked into those green eyes gazing at me with such unquestioning trust. Could I find it within me to kill the light in her eyes. But who else could I tell my troubles to?

"Suha, Papa can no longer afford to send us any more money. The allowance which was meant just for me has to do for both of us until the end of the year.

"Is that *all*?"

A broad smile covered that beautiful face: "I thought you were worried about your studies."

She was still a child, a spoiled child, unaware of how important money was, how you couldn't live without it. What could I say to her?

She fell silent then said, "It's simple, we'll just eat one meal a day. We'll go without breakfast, and for lunch we can buy a loaf of bread and a carton of yogurt."

She laughed and said, "Anyway, it'll keep us slim."

I looked at her with surprise. I was embarrassed at what I had thought. Just who, then, was the spoiled child?

Suha went on: "What do you suppose I ate in the camp?"

I realized that I hadn't asked her anything about the camp. But why? Was it to avoid raking up her painful memories, or to avoid them? Stupid, selfish Saada! Maybe I could forget . . . Acknowledging the miseries of others is not the same as suffering them.

"*Melokhiyya* soup is the cheapest food you can get," I heard her say to me. "I didn't have breakfast or dinner. Every day around noon, I'd buy a plateful of rice and *melokhiyya*. I used to like *melokhiyya*. Now I can't stand it!"

The story about the *melokhiyya* revealed a new Suha, not the Suha who went to parties and dances, the Suha I hated and envied. For the first time in my life, I felt that I had a sister I could involve in my life, that she and I were exploring what I was doing. At the end of the day, when we were tired of studying, we would put our books down, and I'd tell her about school, about the mean-spirited student who had taken out all the books to keep me from doing well on my paper, about the communist professor who had ridiculed me when I said that a small, weak country like Palestine wasn't able to oppose an imperialist power, about my blind classmate who had lost his sight in the army when a bomb had exploded right in front of him and afterwards had decided to go back to school. I kept her up to date with all the news. But I didn't tell her about Amer. I didn't tell her I'd go into the lecture hall, deep in conversation with a friend to keep me from looking up to where I knew he was sitting, with, as I imagined, a mocking look in his eye and a sneer on his lips. I didn't want to talk about him. I didn't want to be reminded. Talking about him would bring back the memory, and the memory would fan the flames of disappointment and embarrassment.

Suha told me about what had happened in Jerusalem just before she left: Arab killing Jew as a warning to the Zionists to let them know they were not welcome; the Zionists taking revenge, killing dozens of innocent Arabs; a bomb placed under a bus seat in an Arab quarter, which exploded with passengers on board; my mother working with other Red Cross volunteers in cleaning and dressing wounds; a bomb left under a seat in a movie theater—the blast tearing apart the movie screen and taking off heads, hands, and legs. Public places were closed, and public transport vehicles were subject to minute searches; people vanished from the streets after sundown, but the number of victims mounted, as did the hatred and the desire for more revenge.

It was only for two months, but during that time I got to know a sister I had lived with for years yet hadn't known at all. I discovered in her someone who was very precious to me and who in years to come was to become a source of happiness and suffering.

She turned her head toward the door when she heard the handle turn.

"Good morning, Sitt Saada. Haifa told me your temperature has gone down and you ate breakfast. Well done!"

The doctor went up to the bed and took hold of her hand, counting her pulse while watching the second hand of his watch. After a minute and a half, he let go of her hand and said, "Pulse is strong and regular, and . . ."

"When can I leave?" she said impatiently.

A broad smile crossed the doctor's face.

"Oh? She doesn't sound as if she's too happy being here with us."

"I'd really like to go home, to my students."

"I understand, but we have to keep you under observation for a while and carry out some other tests to make sure everything's okay. Be patient, Sitt Saada."

He took the chart hanging on the end of the bed by her feet and started examining it. His face didn't reveal a thing. He put back the chart.

"I'll drop by this evening."

He patted her hand and went out. Was he going to come by later because he was worried by something on the chart? Hadn't they been saying she was getting better and everything was okay? Were they lying to her? Again? She looked over at the bouquet of carnations.

⁂

As the last of the applause died away, people started to make their way out toward the main lobby for the intermission. I stood to one side, observing the women in their elegant dresses. Were they there for the music or to show off their clothes and jewelry? As a tall and slender woman passed by me, I looked closely at the stitching on her black dress: a peacock feather on the dress skirt fashioned out of hundreds of tiny pearls and shiny colored sequins. But how could anyone possibly sew all that on?

"Saada! Where have you been hiding?"

I turned around.

"How are you, Ali. I've been around."

"Been around? You don't usually miss a single performance, and I haven't seen you at even one during the past year."

Because of Amer, maybe?

"You know how it is . . . A heavy work load. Then my sister turned up to take her exams."

"Is your sister still here?"

"No, she left."

"What, she went back to Jerusalem?"

⁂

"I need to see you, Saada. Can you come around today?" said my uncle on the phone.

"Is everything okay, Uncle?"

What could be okay when he was calling at seven in the morning and on the weekend as well?

"God willing, everything is fine. Saada, I must see you today. I called early so I'd catch you before you went out."

How strange!

"Is it about my parents?"

"Come around, we can talk about it then."

I got dressed and crept out of the room without waking Suha. Had something happened to my parents? I hurried out to the tram station. But did he say, "God willing, everything is fine," just to keep me calm? Good news always bides its time, while bad news, as the English say, travels fast. But he did say, "God willing, everything is fine." So why was he insisting I come around right away? To tell me good news? The same nagging question kept repeating itself over and over to the monotonous rhythm of the tram. The tram was empty this early in the morning, so I kept my mind busy by watching the houses as they flashed past.

My uncle opened the door. I looked him in the face and said, "Where's Aunt Asma?"

My aunt! My aunt must have had an accident; otherwise she would have been there to greet me.

"She's at the neighbor's. Come in, Saada."

He closed the door behind me.

"This early in the morning?"

He ignored my question.

"Sit down."

He sat down facing me. Silence. Should I ask? If it were good news, he wouldn't be so quiet.

"Saada, I have some bad news."

"My family?"

"Your father."

He fell silent.

"Is he sick?"

He didn't say anything. It had to be worse. I tried not to think about the word. How? When? Why? I started to tremble.

"Is he *dead?*"

There, I had said the word. I had to know.

"Yes, Saada. He had a stroke. We got the letter yesterday evening through the Red Crescent. Asma didn't have the strength to tell you. She's totally distraught. I took it upon myself."

I buried my head in my arms. Papa! My father! I would never ever see him again.

"He died a month ago, but the letter only arrived yesterday."

A month, and I never even knew he was dead and I would never see him again. I had studied, laughed, slept, and Papa was dead. While I had been nursing the wound of a hopeless and foolish love, Papa was dead. He had had a stroke. As well as the pain of loss, I felt a savage hatred for whatever had caused the stroke: Israeli brutality? Arab treachery? The West's betrayal? I didn't stop to think or reason. I only felt anger and hatred and loathing . . . and deep despair.

৯৹

"What's wrong Saada? Why don't you say anything?"

Say anything? Oh yes, Ali. What was he asking me? Then I remembered.

"No, of course I can't go back to Jerusalem. My father died, and Mama collected all her belongings and went back to her country. Suha's with her now in Beirut."

"Your father died? God will provide for your well being."

The bell announcing that the performance was about to continue came to my rescue. He held out his hand.

"I'll see you soon, God willing."

He hurried inside. I couldn't concentrate on a Brahms symphony when he had picked the scab off the wound, so I left the hall and went outside to walk in the warm June night.

I walked that day, too. I walked and walked, unable to keep the tears from streaming down my face, like a veil through which I saw people moving ghost-like around me, shadowy faces, cars. I looked down at my feet—the sidewalk stretched on and on, dark, nondescript, mournful. The May sun warmed my wet cheeks. Papa's birthday was on the twentieth of May. Suha's exams ended on the twentieth of May. I couldn't tell her. She had to take her exams. She had to pass them . . . Where was I going? Twenty million souls in this city, twenty million strangers. No, I was the stranger, a stranger since the day I first registered at the university. A stranger, alone, waiting for Papa, Papa who was afraid of getting lost, who didn't really know me, who had brought me to Cairo. Tears streaming from my eyes, I visualized the scene while I was waiting outside the main university entrance. Half-past eight, nine. I was starting to worry about him. He was usually punctual. When a tram stopped at the entrance, spitting out droves of students and employees, I searched through them, at first with hope, then with anxiety. Finally I saw him. He was being shoved from behind, left and right, by dozens of young men. He was holding onto one of the straps that hung from the tram ceiling to avoid losing his balance. The pressure behind him built up until he lost his grip and was carried along by the wave down the steps and onto the sidewalk. The wave hemmed in on him from every direction, but still he kept his balance. He held his tarboush on with one hand and pressed his glasses firmly against his nose with the other. He stood there trying to collect himself, the sweat pouring from his forehead and cheeks. How much he loved me. How much he had put up with just for me . . .

I phoned Suha.

"I won't be home until this evening. I'm going to study with a friend of mine in the university library."

When I came back at nine, Suha was asleep. I threw myself down on the bed, exhausted from walking around the streets the entire day.

৯৭

"Sitt Saada?"

Maybe she's so tired because of her illness. She's not opening her eyes.

The nurse would give her her medication, if that's what she was there for, even if she were asleep. But she could hear the nurse walking off and talking to someone outside.

"I'm sorry, sir, but she's asleep. Do you want to leave your name?"

Who was it, she wondered. Him? She heard footsteps; then the door closed. But why did she think it was him? Because he sent a bouquet, a bouquet of carnations?

5

Ali called me the next day.

"How's school?"

"My final exam's tomorrow."

"Why don't we meet afterwards to celebrate. I finished mine yesterday."

He was already there when I turned up at the main zoo entrance at half-past one. It was extremely hot. My sweat-soaked gray blouse was clinging to my back and perspiration was pouring from my face. But I was in a good mood.

"How was it?"

"Easier than I thought. I was really lucky, Ali. Yesterday I was studying the development of poetry from the Jahiliyya to the Abbasid period and the very subject came up in the exam."

"Great. So you're sure to keep up your outstanding grades."

"It's only one exam out of many."

"Less of the false modesty, Saada. You know yourself . . ."

Then he gave me a searching look and said, "All this studying is wearing you out. Or maybe . . ."

He fell silent. Maybe he was afraid of reminding me about my father's death. He knew nothing about my anxiety over Suha or about Amer.

"Let's go in."

He steered me to the ticket window. Yes, "the monkey" had lost its fat these past few months. Wasn't that why Ali was taking an interest in me now, or was it just to comfort me about my father? And what about Salem? I had been in school with him for three years and he had never paid me any attention before. Not to me nor anyone else.

Whenever Salem tried to pick on me, I felt giddy and lightheaded. Salem, the high-and-mighty, who didn't rub shoulders with anyone. He was the only one who came to school in his own car. His parties, his exploits, his lifestyle were all everyone ever talked about in class. They made remarks, snippy comments—they were jealous . . . Salem asked me to give him some background on a lecture he had missed. I was so overcome by giddiness I accepted. That occasion was followed by others. Then he asked me, "Do you want to come to a party?"

"Not like everyone else, different"? I felt the same jolt of fear when I was running, getting away from Amer . . . The one who wasn't like everyone else, who was different. I turned him down. I turned him down and cut off all contact with him.

But Ali? Ali was "different, not like everyone else," like me. Like me?

I had forgotten how hot it was as we strolled through the zoo. I had forgotten how hungry I was.

"Are you going to go to Lebanon for the vacation, too?"

His sudden question cut dead our talk about studies, professors, exams.

"No, I can't afford it. I'm going to stay at my aunt's until the dorm reopens in October. It's okay for you, you're going back to your own country."

"It'll be your country, too, as soon as you finish college."

I smiled. It was true. His parents were from different countries—he shared the characteristics of both. He belonged to two countries. Did I think about belonging? The chameleon? I laughed.

"Do you remember the time you thought I was Egyptian?"

He smiled: "And now you're adding another to your Palestinian and Egyptian identity—Lebanese."

What did I know about Lebanon? Snow, high mountains, not at all like Palestine or Egypt. Spectacular natural scenery, the hallowed cedars. Unique Phoenicean and Roman remains. I had read all about it in books, seen it in photographs. Was this a country's identity?

"Tell me about Lebanon."

"Not before we've eaten, I'm dying of hunger!"

He looked at his watch.

"Saada, it's half-past two!"

He turned around and set off at a brisk pace for the zoo restaurant. I followed behind him.

❧

We strolled along the bank of the Nile just before sunset. The sun's temper had cooled, and the wide pavement was packed with people out walking.

Our date at the zoo three weeks earlier was the first of what became a daily routine while we waited for the exam results. I would meet him at Biba bridge at five, and we would walk until half-past seven. I would then return to the dorm, and he would go back to his apartment. While we walked, he would tell me about Beirut. It was much smaller than Cairo. It didn't have the grand department stores Cairo had, nor its trendy shops, wide streets, or European-style cafés. But it was "passable." It possessed a particular charm with its narrow, winding streets and sea-front quarters, its traditional coffee-houses looking out on the sea, and its people. He told me about the people: their houses and hearts open to every stranger, their liveliness and *joie de vivre*.

"Did your government put you in charge of tourist advertising?" I asked, laughing.

He replied in all seriousness, "*You* asked me to tell you about Lebanon . . . That's Lebanon."

"Lebanon? Beirut more like."

He told me about the country estate up in the mountains: how his uncle would take a stick to the boys he caught stealing grapes from his vineyard; about old Sara who would seize any visit by a stranger to recite all the poems she knew; Maryam who flouted morality and tradition by becoming the mistress of Asad, a married man. Well, that was what wagging tongues were saying.

He told me all about his father and his medical supplies store and his three sisters.

"You're the only boy?"

"Yes, and as soon as I get back with a diploma in engineering, Mama's going to marry me off."

"And you don't mind her marrying you off to someone?" I blurted out the question without thinking and immediately regretted it.

"I'm not thinking about that right now. I've still got one more year to go."

Was he being sincere, or was he avoiding the question? More so, what right did I have meddling in his personal life? The wound Amer had inflicted had healed, so why should I put myself in a situation where I could be wounded again? Ali was Lebanese like Mama. He was like me—he was different. He wasn't making friends with me so he could take advantage of me, just because I didn't happen to be a female from his country . . .

I told him about the city I was from (Would I ever see it again?): Jerusalem was even smaller than Beirut. It didn't have Cairo's palaces, parks, restaurants, or bridges.

"But it's our holy city, Ali. The path on which Christ bore his cross, the garden of Gethsemane where he said his last prayer, the Church of the Resurrection, al-Aqsah, the Dome on the Rock, Ali, the most beautiful mosques in the world. A city holy to both you and me."

I said enthusiastically, "It's beautiful, really beautiful. The houses are made from a pink-colored stone I've never seen except in Jerusalem.

Suddenly I stopped at a flower seller.

"Do you see those carnations? They're the same color as the houses in Jerusalem."

I gazed at the bouquet of carnations in silence, thinking about the ugly concrete apartments the immigrant Jews had built in Jerusalem. The man held out the bouquet of carnations.

"God bless you, ya Sitt, ya Afandi. Are not these flowers as pink as the lady's cheeks?"

My cheeks turned from pink to a deep red.

"Do you like carnations?" Ali asked.

"It's my favorite flower."

He bought me the bouquet. I described to him the Dome on the Rock and the wonderful mosaics on its outer walls, the Church of the Resurrection, and the narrow alleyways of the Old City where we used to walk along the Stations of the Cross which commemorate the suffering of Christ. I mentioned Palm Sunday; then I fell silent.

"Palm Sunday?" he asked.

Since my silence continued, he asked again, "What about Palm Sunday? Why did you go quiet?"

It all poured out in a rush: "Your memories, Ali, are part of your present, part of your future. I've cut myself off from my past, totally cut myself off."

Ali stopped dead and stared at me. Was it a look of pity or ridicule? All of a sudden he smiled and said, "Have you forgotten your mother is in Lebanon, waiting for you? Don't feel so sorry for yourself! Don't exaggerate. Nothing can wipe out the past. The proof is that you're talking about it!"

Was my self-pity an attempt to gain his sympathy and attention? Stupid girl! How could anyone not in my position understand my feelings, my feelings for my land, my past, or everything else. I quickly dismissed the thought.

The exam results we had been waiting for came out. He was now going back to Lebanon. I was going to live at my aunt's.

"Are you leaving tomorrow then?"

"Yes. Is there anything I can take back to your family for you?"

"A letter. I'll write it tonight."

"I'll drop by early tomorrow and pick it up . . . and say good-bye."

Finally, when we came to the park gate in front of the student dorm, I held out my hand to shake farewell. He suddenly seized it with both his hands and squeezed it. I could feel the heat from his hands flow through my body. My heart started to beat faster and faster, almost deafening me; then he suddenly drew me to him and kissed me on the head.

"Ali, we're in the street!"

I pushed him away from me. Had anyone seen us? Thank God it was dark—it hid both me and my blushing face.

"So what if we're in the street? Is it against the law to kiss a friend good-bye?"

My heart seemed to stop. Was that just a friendly embrace, just a friendly kiss? Was I imagining it all? I was afraid of myself, so I turned around and walked off rapidly into the park without looking back.

A friendly embrace? But it was so passionate. Had he lied, lied about what he told me about himself, his love for music, literature, just like my own? An engineer who could recite the poetry of Tarafa, Abu Nuwas, and Mutanabbi, and who, like me, loved Hakeem's plays. Was it all just to win me over, to seduce me?

Hadn't I learned my lesson? Wasn't I happy with him, comfortable with him? Had he also lied? Why did I start trembling when he hugged me? My whole body had started trembling. I was tossing and turning in bed. Was it only friendship he felt? What did I feel? Was he another Amer, or was he "not like everyone else, different"? Did he always say good-bye to his friends like that whether they were male or female? Female friends? I was the only one he had been seeing. For that month, I hadn't been out with Samiya, Atayet, Baha, Anis. I really liked my friends. I had only seen them at university, bumped into them by chance. What were they saying about me? What did they think of me? Fickle? Unreliable? A chameleon! All I really had were my friends. But didn't he say he was a friend. And me, when was I ever troubled by friendship? Friendship? Or a passionate embrace? The warmth which flowed from him to me? Or was it only in me? Friendship? Another Amer?

I still hadn't come up with any answers to my questions when dawn peered through the gaps in the curtains. I got up and gathered together my clothes and books to move to my aunt's.

6

"She's been asleep all day."

"It's a good sign."

"Yes, but she's not really eating. She had breakfast but hasn't had anything since."

"Did she eat her lunch?"

"I tried to wake her but didn't have any luck. I left it by her bed and came back half an hour later. She was still asleep, and the food was cold."

"What did the doctor say?" Suha draped her coat on the hanger on the back of the door and propped a parcel wrapped in thick brown paper against the wall.

"He saw her this morning. He said he was going to come back in the evening." Suha drew up the chair to the bed.

"Didn't he say anything?" she asked the nurse.

Seeing the patient moving in bed, the nurse placed a finger to her lips and motioned with her other hand that she would speak to Suha outside afterwards. She then left the room.

Suha sat there, watching her sleeping sister. *Her face loses all its attractiveness when the gleam in her small dancing eyes is hidden. Her vitality, her love for life, her intelligence are all in her eyes. Her face isn't like Modigliani's faces. Her intelligence!*

৵

"Saada Rayyis's sister?"

I nodded in reply; then came the familiar response, a response all the teachers had made since I was at school: "Are you intelligent and hardworking like her?"

Like her? Intelligent? Who would have wanted to make friends with her just because she was intelligent? She was always alone, alone with her books. So arrogant! How I hated her! Our teachers—it never occurred to any of them that comparing me with Saada only increased my contempt, loathing, and resentment.

Suha felt a wave of compassion surge in her heart. She stared at the fragile face before her; how pale and thin it looked. It was as pale as Papa's face that time she had lied: "I lost my report card."

Saada, quite full of herself, asked him for her report card back and shot me a look of triumph. As usual, Saada's grades were excellent. As usual, my grades were dismal. Papa praised her, then turned to me. I didn't dare give him my report card. However hard I tried, I would never be as good as her. Why bother? If they were comparing me to her, let them! I would only be me. I remember his anger welling up bright red against his pale skin.

"You lost it?"

He took off his leather belt. I froze; then I ran. I hid behind the table, but Papa shouted, "Saada, get her for me!"

Saada, of course, jumped to obey. I was caught between her and Papa. The leather belt rained down blow after blow on my legs.

"Make sure you don't lose your report card again . . ."

Whack!

"Or any other report cards."

Whack!

"Or books."

He continued to hit me. I gritted my teeth, forcing back the tears, the cries of pain. I didn't move—I stood still as a statue. Eventually, Mama intervened: "That's enough, Shafiq. I think she understands. She's learned her lesson."

She grabbed his arm and forced it away from me. I ran off to my room, closed the door, and threw myself on my bed. Only then did my suppressed pain, humiliation, and tears explode, feeding my hatred for Saada, for Papa. She was his favorite.

"What are you thinking about?"

"You're awake?"

Her sister's voice brought her back to the present. She got up and kissed her on the forehead.

"How are you feeling?"

"Much better, thank you. How long have you been here? What's the time?"

Suha glanced at her watch: "Three-thirty . . . The nurse tells me you're not eating. Saada, how do you expect to get better?"

However much Suha tried, it just wasn't possible for her beautiful face to look harsh. Saada smiled weakly as she gazed into her sister's face.

"I just need sleep. Didn't Mama say when Nadia was born that sleep was more important to a child than eating?"

"But you're not a child!"

"I feel like I'm a child again!"

You or me? Suha smiled, then got up and brought her sister the parcel.

"I did this painting for you. If you don't like it, I've got others."

She started to take off the paper wrapped around it. When she had freed the painting from its packaging, she stood back from the foot of the bed, holding it up for Saada to see. The surprise left the sick woman at a loss for words. She couldn't contain her emotions, so she closed her eyes while tears ran down in silence.

"Suha!"

Her voice was choked. What had made her want to remember that now? What had made her bring it up again? Maybe because Suha was a rock, a rock firmly rooted in the ground. She wasn't a chameleon like her. The chameleon loves rocks, lives on them, gets it warmth from them. And the rocks? Well, they love the chameleon and lend it their color.

"Don't you like it? You haven't said a word."

She took refuge in her silence until she had regained her composure; then she opened her eyes and focused them on the painting.

"Of course I like it!"

Saada gazed at the pink stone house, which loomed out from among the branches of a pine tree. It had a red tiled roof, and nestling between the tree trunks was a large balcony where, afternoons, their father would sit in his rocking chair while she and Suha rode their bicycles back and forth, back and forth until their father shouted out, "Okay, that's enough. You two are driving me crazy!"

"What do you remember about our house in Jerusalem?"

"Why, have you forgotten?"

Suha's look of disapproval wounded her, so she said, smiling, "Many are the houses a man lives in, but his heart is always for the first."

Suha made no reply. Instead she rewrapped the painting and said, "I'll get it framed for you."

She looked at her watch: "I need to get going, Saada. I have to pick Nadia up from school. Promise me you'll eat your dinner. Promise me now, won't you."

In Suha's eyes was a look of request and command.

"I promise."

Suha leaned over her sister, kissed her, then left.

In two hours time they would bring her dinner. The doctor would come. She closed her eyes.

✒

But his heart is always for the first, as mine is for the house where I was born, which has since been torn down. But before it was: "Saada, we're going to rent a car and take a look around Jerusalem. Come with us. Some friends of mine are doing the tourist thing in the Old City. You know, al-Aqsah, the Dome on the Rock, the Church of the Resurrection."

"Thank you, but no."

Did I want to peer through fences and barbed-wire at Jerusalem, which had once been my Jerusalem? Did I want to visit as a tourist what had been part of my past, while being denied the part in which I was still alive?

"Aren't you just dying to see your old home?"

But his heart is always for the first. Was my house still there? Who was living in it now? I blanked out those thoughts. In my mind was the image of the British minister defending his government, justifying the withdrawal from Palestine which left the Arabs and Jews "at each others throats."

"The Americans and the postwar Marshall Plan are essential to bring an end to our economic crisis and food shortages."

Astonished, the journalist asked, "Did America stipulate the withdrawal?"

The Englishman replied frostily, "President Truman was seeking reelection. He needed the Jewish vote in the United States. This was their condition."

The journalist said, "But didn't you sell out what wasn't yours in the beginning?"

The journalist's naiveté surprised me, and it reminded me of a certain history lesson: If it was possible to *take back* something that wasn't theirs in the first place, what could prevent them from *selling it out*?

&

Suha preferred to walk home. The cold air was refreshing after the stuffy hospital room and her recent conversation with the nurse: "We can't be absolutely sure at the moment. We removed the tumor and the surrounding tissue. Only time will tell."

"What do the statistics say about conditions like hers."

The nurse smiled: "Statistics? They don't mean much. I don't want to frighten you, but I don't want to build up false hopes either. Even though statistics state that 75 percent of cases similar to your sister's recover, she may be among the 25 percent who don't. I'm sorry, but I don't want to mislead you."

She choked back a momentary feeling of disappointment, then asked, "But do you really know?"

"Of course not. We're confident she's in the 75 percent, but we have to warn you so you can put her affairs in order or help her do that without letting her know anything . . . That is, if what we hope doesn't happen happens."

"Thank you," she replied automatically.

She left. Thank you? For such worrying and frightening news? But was it the nurse's fault? Somebody else's fault? Mama's? The doctors were saying cancer wasn't hereditary. Some of them were saying that. Others were saying cancer was hereditary. Had Mama passed it on to Saada? Mama had paid for her sins, for all her sins, if she were guilty. Her beautiful, statuesque mother, her long, thick hair rolled in a bun above her swan-like neck, her pale, fresh, clear complexion which was flawless except for some lines at the side of her mouth and eyes. Or was the cause of those wrinkles her eternal smile, a smile that had defied homesickness, widowhood, and her leaving her country? Then it had succumbed to illness. In her mind's eye she saw the skeletal form of her mother slumped in bed, her cheek bones and nose protruding from under the transparent, yellowish skin. The only glimmer of life, a life like a dying flame, appeared in her green eyes which seemed so much larger because she was so thin. They couldn't move her. Cancer had eaten into her bones, leaving nothing but an empty shell. Since her body was covered in a rash of ulcerated sores, they didn't want to cause her any more pain. Ointment was no use. There was no effective treatment for them, so they bandaged them with sterile dressings to stop the flesh from macerating. And maybe the looks from those green eyes were not just of agony, but of blame, because it was only she who was dying, while the world remained and life went on. Strange, brooding looks as if from another world.

"Mama, what is it? Do you want something?"

The only reply came in the form of those silent, brooding looks, looks which had haunted her to that day.

A shiver ran through her body. Was this going to be Saada's fate, too? Suha drew her coat around her. It was bitterly cold even though it was only November. She smiled wryly. If it hadn't been for November, she would never have become an artist. The words of her father came back to her: "Don't hate something—it might be good for you." She hugged the picture tighter against her side and quickened her pace to keep out the cold.

7

The bus was parked by the sidewalk. The driver was on the roof while the assistant handed suitcases and belongings up to him. A group of young and old men and women stood nearby, the din of conversation and laughter rising from them. The driver looked at his watch and shouted above the hubbub, "Come on, it's time to go!"

Hugs, kisses, farewells. Mothers tried in vain to hide their tears. The young men and women boarded the bus.

"Don't forget to wear your coat when you go out at night. Paris is chilly at night, even in summer."

"Nuha, call Monsieur Duval as soon as you get there and say hello to him from me."

"You do know when you're due back, don't you?"

"Papa, I've told you a thousand times we're going to be gone for exactly three weeks!"

The passengers took their seats. Faces peered out from behind the windows. The bus pulled away, necks craned, and hands waved in reply to the handkerchiefs from the sidewalk. After a short while, it disappeared from view.

Half an hour or so later they were at the airport. Each of them, suitcase in hand, lined up in front of the check-in desk. Their suitcases were weighed, then rolled through a hole to be loaded onto the airplane. Nerves only settled after they passed the window of public security and descended the stairs to the departure lounge.

"What are you reading?"

The question made her jump so she looked up from her book. A young man, slim, medium height, about her age.

"*The Beginning and the End* by Naguib Mahfouz."

"Any good?"

"I've just started it."

To cut the conversation dead with the young man she didn't know, she went back to reading her book.

He ignored her indifference and introduced himself: "Anwar Shihaab. I'm a doctor. I'm in the final year of training as a surgeon."

Without being invited, he sat down beside her. She thought to herself, "How I hate these young men who think they're God's gift to women! They think they're the center of attention. Just because he's a doctor! Mister Wonderful!!"

She didn't reply, nor did she introduce herself—she just continued to read. The only problem was she found his presence irritating, and that ruined her concentration. Why had he chosen her especially? Should she sit somewhere else? His voice then broke through her confusion: "Won't you allow me to introduce myself?"

Should she reply or ignore him? He was going to be her travel companion after all. She hesitated, then said dryly, "Suha Rayyis."

"Are you a student?"

"I work in a bank."

He fell silent. Maybe her terse reply had made him realize that she didn't want to start a conversation. But it seemed that he didn't get the message.

"Is this your first trip to Paris?" But before she had time to reply he added, "It's my first time away from Lebanon."

"Me too."

"Even though you are working?"

She smiled in spite of herself and said, "It's because I do actually work. Do you think I just make money to travel and have a good time?"

"I do apologize, Suha," he said, his face turning slightly red. "I spoke without thinking."

A renewed silence. She went back to her book but wasn't able to switch her thoughts from the young man who was sitting next to her . . .

"Will all passengers on the Middle-East Airlines flight to Paris please proceed to gate number eight," the stewardess's voice rang out, and there was a mass rush to the gate. Suha found herself at the end of the line with Anwar Shihaab still at her side. Was he intending to stick with her? She ignored him and fixed her gaze on the back of the person in front of her. When she climbed on board the shuttle to the plane, she looked around for a seat near Zina.

"Are you opposed to my sitting by you in the plane, too?"

"Yes, I am."

Anwar disappeared.

❧

The following morning, they assembled in the dining room and listened to the tour guide spell out the program for the first day . . .

❧

In the Louvre, Suha stood contemplating the *Mona Lisa*.

"I can't understand why this painting is so famous," she said to Zina. "There are far more beautiful paintings in here."

"I totally agree with you," Suha heard from behind her.

She didn't need to turn around to know whose voice it was. She felt a wave of anger overcome her. Why didn't he get the message! Without bothering to reply, she turned her back to him and moved away from the painting.

They visited other museums, Les Invalides, public parks, places of historical interest. They went to films, plays, the Comédie-Française. However, when the guide suggested they go to a concert they all declined, all except Suha, Zina, Sameer, and Anwar. Not Anwar again! But then she remonstrated with herself—surely he had the right to go where he liked.

"In that case, I'll leave the tickets and transportation to the concert up to you so I can work out an alternative program with the rest of the group."

On the way back, the conversation revolved around what music they liked, the records they had bought, and the concerts they had been to. Why had she thought him such an idiot?

Two days later: "How would you like to go to a concert tonight?"

Noticing her hesitation, Anwar added, "It's free. There are certain

64

churches you can go to and hear concerts for free, and they're just as good as the other concerts."

Should she say no because of who was asking? No, this time she was the one who was being the idiot. It was just that the other two who had been to the concert with them had made other plans, so it was just the two of them who were going.

After that concert came other concerts, a movie none of the others wanted to watch, an exhibition no one else wanted to see except Rana and Shadiya.

"Do you like sports as well?" Anwar asked.

He thought it unlikely she'd be willing to pay all that money to see a game at Roland Garros.

"Only tennis."

"I'm a soccer fan myself."

He paused, then said, "I'm a man of plebeian tastes."

"A plebeian doctor and an aristocratic junior bank employee!" she said ironically, and he laughed.

Before they knew it, the trip was coming to an end and it was time to go back.

"Do you think Mama will like this blouse?"

"I've forgotten to buy a present for my uncle!"

"Just how much money did you bring with you that you can afford presents for all your relatives, even your uncle?"

"My uncle is different. He doesn't go anywhere without coming back with presents for everyone."

They were looking forward to their return with anticipation.

৵

"In five minutes we will be landing at Beirut International Airport. The weather is fair and the temperature is seventy-five degrees. We hope that you have enjoyed traveling with us on Middle-East Airlines and that we will see you again in the near future."

People craned their necks to look through the windows.

"Look, there's the golf course. You can see the players."

"And the sailboats on the sea."

No sooner had the wheels touched the ground than everyone stood up, ignoring the pilot's instructions and the signs above the seats.

Holding out their passports, they lined up in front of the booths of the public security officials, but their heads were looking past them.

"See how much my little sister's grown in the last few weeks!"

"Uncle, Uncle! My uncle from the Gulf is here!"

"Isn't anyone waiting for you?"

"Sure, my sister."

He noticed that she was smiling and waving at a young woman with a round brown face and long black hair from behind the glass partition of the arrivals section. "She doesn't resemble her sister in the least," was what he was thinking.

While waiting for the bags to arrive, he asked her, "When can I see you?"

She immediately answered, "The trip is over, and we're going back to our own particular worlds."

"Does that stop us from being friends, then?"

She said nothing in reply. Her suitcases had arrived, so she picked them up, said good-bye to whichever of her companions happened to be near her, and walked off.

Was she so high and mighty because she was beautiful? Did all the time they had spent together mean nothing to her? She seemed to treat it as though it had been nothing!

"Anwar, isn't that your suitcase?"

Saleem's voice brought him back to reality. He picked his suitcase up and left the airport.

ॐ

As soon as Saada came in the door the telephone started to ring. "Hello?"

"Is that Miss Saada Rayyis?"

When she replied, "Yes," the voice continued, "You don't know me, my name's Anwar Shihaab. I was with your sister Suha on the Paris trip."

He fell silent. She was expecting him to go on talking, but when she didn't hear him say anything else, she said, "Yes?"

He paused again, then said, "Could I meet with you?"

His question took her momentarily by surprise; then she replied, "Of course. I'm at home right now if you'd like to see me today. Do you know where we live?"

Saada gave him the address and hung up. What did he want? Suha had never mentioned him before. But then again, she never talked about anybody she met. It wasn't her way. All she ever talked about was Zina. Saada went into the kitchen to prepare dinner. She placed the pan of water on the stove, sprinkled salt in it, then opened the pantry door and took out the macaroni. It was curious he was so insistent on speaking with her. What did he want? She got the tomatoes and cucumbers from the fridge, took a knife from the drawer, and started to cut up the vegetables. When she had just finished preparing the bowl of salad the doorbell rang.

She opened the door to see a slim young man of medium height standing before her. Large gentle eyes peered out from behind his glasses, and thin lips appeared from under his mustache.

"Anwar? Please come in."

She led him to the parlor.

"How do you take your coffee?"

"Excuse me, but I don't want coffee or anything else. I've bothered you enough as it is, and I don't want to take up any more of your time."

"Well okay then. Suit yourself! Suha will be back in half an hour or so. No doubt she'll be pleased you're here to see her."

She watched his expression to see if her words had any effect. He blushed slightly, his upper lip trembled, and that was all. He sat opposite her in silence. He sat there, his gaze fixed on the rug under his feet. She watched him and waited. She didn't know whether to try talking or just stay silent. She stole a glance at her watch.

"I was a friend of Suha's in Paris."

Maybe he had noticed her gesture.

"You told me that already."

"Yes, and . . . and . . ."

"And?"

"I don't know why now she doesn't want to see me."

She knew, but she said, "So, forget her. You can't make someone go out with you who doesn't want to."

He hesitated, then said, "Yes I know, but we had so much in common, and we were getting on really well with each other, and I don't understand why everything changed just because we're back in Beirut! If I upset her or hurt her in some way, I want to apologize. I want to know."

She felt sorry for the young man before her. What could she tell him?

"I don't think so. At least, Suha never said anything to me."

Then he broke down: "I tried to forget her, but I couldn't. I never thought that just a few weeks could change someone so. They changed me. While I was at the hospital, with patients, in front of books, all I could think of was Suha. I remember everything she said, everything she did, her laugh, the way she moved, spoke . . . Please, I beg you Sitt Saada, you've got to help me!"

Help him?

"How? What can I possibly do?"

He looked up into her eyes, and she saw an echo of the desperation that was in his voice.

He said, "Suha told me how much she loves you, trusts you. Try to find out from her why. Right up to when the trip ended we shared so much in common—films, music, even sport.

He gave her a weak smile, and Saada smiled in response. She wanted to tell him life was not just films, music, and sport, but she said, "I'll talk to her, if that's what you want, but I can't promise

I'll get her to tell me how she feels, or get her to agree to see you."

He rose to his feet and said in an agitated tone, "It's important that I know, that I know . . . Thank you, Miss Saada, thank you."

He held out his hand to shake good-bye and strode to the door. It seemed as though he wanted to leave before Suha got back, but he suddenly stopped, turned toward Saada, and said, "When can you let me know?"

Restless movement, constant hurry belied the calm in his eyes.

"Give me your phone number, I'll be in touch."

❦

To hide her unease, Saada asked her sister to come to the kitchen with her. She handed Suha an onion to chop; then she put the meat in the pan to fry in the butter.

"Anwar Shihaab came by to see me."

She looked at Suha to observe the effect of what she had just said. Suha stopped chopping, and without looking up, answered, "I didn't realize you knew him."

Suha's face had turned a deep red, so Saada replied, "I didn't, but he introduced himself to me."

When Suha didn't comment, she continued: "He came about you. He came to ask me to ask you why you are so determined to cut him off completely, after what was between you in Paris."

Suha suddenly looked up at her sister, her eyes brimming with hate and anger.

"There was nothing between us. If he told you anything else, he's a liar!"

Was she angry or just embarrassed? However, Saada said quietly, "He didn't tell me anything and he didn't strike me as a liar. In fact, Suha, he struck me as a straightforward and honest young man, really quite troubled by your anger toward him, and he wants to know why."

Suha failed to respond, so she asked, "Why do you refuse to see him?"

Suha remained obstinate in her silence. Her sister went on: "You know I don't normally interfere in your affairs, but I felt sorry for him. He's fonder of you than you think."

Since Suha was still maintaining a guarded silence. Saada thought for a moment then asked, "Aren't you still going out with Mounir?"

Suha appeared ruffled and said nervously, "Why do you ask?"

"Frankly, I think that's the reason for your breaking off with everyone else. And frankly, he doesn't compare to Anwar at all."

Suha erupted angrily: "That's none of your business! . . . You don't know Mounir, nor do you know Anwar!"

"It's my business if my only sister's happiness and future is at stake," Saada replied in a calm and sympathetic voice. "Maybe . . ."

"Please, I don't want to talk about it!"

"Let me say what I want to say," Saada said in the same sympathetic tone. "After that we'll never bring up the subject again. I don't object to Mounir, except that he's quite a lot older than you. When you're a middle-aged woman in her forties, he'll be an old man and might even be senile."

"Don't . . ."

"Suha, please, let me finish what have to say. So, what is Mounir's future? All he'll ever be is an ordinary bank employee. He doesn't have the right qualifications to get a promotion. You deserve better than him. After a few years, you'll find yourself with an old man you don't respect. You won't love him and . . ."

"Who said I was going to marry him!"

"So, you will have wasted the best years of your life on him. It might be he's fooling himself, thinking you love him, staking his future on you. But is he to blame? Look at you, you're too good for him! I'm not saying that because you're my sister, but because I love you. You alone know how much."

She stopped to let Suha take in what she had said and to let her think it over. A minute or two later she continued: "Suha, my dear, maybe you're refusing to see Anwar so no one says you change boyfriends like you change clothes. But what people say isn't that important when it's your whole life in the balance. Give yourself the opportunity to get to know other men, someone better than Mounir, someone you can depend on."

A heavy silence settled between the sisters. Minutes ticked by, then Saada said, "Isn't it about time you started thinking seriously about your future, Suha? I'm waiting, and not too patiently, to become an aunt, for my sister to have children."

"Why don't you get married yourself if you want children?" Suha retorted.

She didn't notice Saada trembling slightly, nor her face turning pale. Saada threw her arms around Suha's shoulders and kissed her lightly on the cheek.

"Do think seriously about what I said, Suha. I'll never bring up this subject again."

৯৹

Nine months later Anwar Shihaab completed his training as a surgeon. They got married and moved to the Gulf where Nadia was born.

8

Nine years the hospital, patients, operations filled his life.

He came back one evening:

"Suha, don't leave that box of thumbtacks open. Only today an eight-year-old child had an operation to remove an inch-long safety pin he swallowed. It's a miracle he didn't choke to death."

And on another evening:

"Today I had a child come in with a swollen nose which was giving off this awful smell. His parents had noticed this awful smell when he breathed out, but they only did something about it when the nose started to swell up and they couldn't stand the smell any longer."

"What caused it?"

"A garbanzo bean got stuck up his nose!"

She enjoyed his anecdotes of the operations he performed, the stories about the patients and nurses, and his conversations with them and the other doctors for a year, two years. Then she started to feel how small she had become.

"I'm going to get a job."

"My colleagues' wives don't work. Your husband's a doctor remember. And what about Nadia?"

She fell silent. Silence filled the emptiness. Sometimes it was filled by the strains of a Beethoven symphony or a Mozart sonata. One evening when he came home: "Suha, please, I'm exhausted. Turn the music off."

Was this the Anwar of old, the Anwar of Paris? When he came back, silence filled the emptiness, and unhappiness filled the silence . . . or his stories, anecdotes, operations, conversations. Stories about another world. She divided her attention between that and her world, a world of triviality, unhappiness, silence, and emptiness. From within that world she would watch him talking to her. Didn't he realize she might be unhappy? Didn't he feel that he had changed? Or that she had changed? Did he ever wonder what she was thinking, what she was feeling? Did he ever notice how cold and silent she was to him? Did he? Was he even curious or interested? He only seemed to care about himself, his work, his world. His world? Did she know what really went on in his world? She didn't want to think about it. She was suffering enough already.

In response, she erected the same wall of indifference which surrounded him, and which protected his inner self, a wall which divided the two worlds. She began to voice her thoughts: "You spend all your time working, so why can't I work as well? I'm tired of all the visits, the invitations, the dinner parties."

In the end he was satisfied as long as she wasn't working for someone else. The long hours of her days grew shorter when she flung herself into studying the history of art, the principles of drawing, working in water colors and oils. She experimented with layering on paper and canvas.

"I'll pay you back every penny I owe you . . . As soon as I sell something."

Smiling, he gave her money: "I don't need it. I just want you to enjoy yourself."

The remark got under her skin—his work was serious and hers was just a hobby! She spent hour after hour painting, tearing it up, doing it over again, changing this, changing that. She took the least time possible on the housework (thanks to Babu) then she would barricade herself in the room, "her studio" as she herself called it. To him, to Nadia, to her friends, it was her room. The studio was where an artist worked—she would become an artist! She painted, tore it up, did it over again, changed this, changed that. She read books about art, studied famous paintings, and painted and painted.

Days . . . months . . . years.

"The club has agreed to let me use one of their rooms for free."

"One of their rooms? What are you going to do there?"

She raised her voice to cover her wildly beating heart: "I'm going put on an exhibition of my paintings!"

"For whom?"

Was he making fun of her or was he just asking?

"For whoever who wants to buy them."

"What, you're going to sell them?"

His disapproval made her furious. Did he doubt her talent? Was he trying to put down her determination? Her hesitation, her fear, vanished before her rage.

"Why not?"

"Because you're not an artist!"

"Whoever buys them will consider me an artist."

"The only people who'll buy them will be friends or acquaintances, either out of embarrassment or to support you, and . . ."

"I'm not telling friends or acquaintances," she said angrily. "I'm going to hang them in the club, and only people who are curious enough or who love art will come to see them. I've asked Samaan to sell them. I won't be there, so no one will be embarrassed for me or feel obliged to say something kind."

"Samaan?"

"Samaan Daroub, the club director."

He looked at her in surprise. When did she get to be so self-confident, so single-minded and independent? The poor thing, her own conceit had blinded her. He winced at the thought of how disappointed she would be when reality finally struck.

❧

"You have to stay, Sitt Suha."

"No, I'm letting you handle it. That should be enough."

Her eyes flew from one painting to another; then she went up to two that were leaning slightly to the left and straightened them.

"What if anybody wants to know who the artist is or wants to be introduced to her?"

"The paintings are signed."

"But you're not even using your real name."

"Are they buying the painting or the name?"

She began to gather up her stuff to leave before the club visitors started to arrive. Samaan Daroub smiled—a naive amateur, he thought to himself.

"Last year, people were falling over themselves to buy Nasser Abdullah's book only because they knew his name from the papers, radio, and television. It was the first book he had written, so there was nothing to go on to say it was any good. They were buying the name, not the book."

His story had no effect. She was as stubborn as ever.

"You can't tell if a book is any good before you read it. A painting is right there in front of you. You either like it or you don't."

She hurried off outside. Samaan only wished she had had the

74

courage and confidence to stay, to see their expressions and hear their comments. Samiya Safa—who ever heard of her before? He smiled wryly. There was no way she could endure their criticism. She was unknown. Everybody around there who carried a brush thought he or she was an artist. Just like all the rest who wouldn't show up. He looked at the primitive figures—what a clash of colors! Was that art? She had rushed off to get away from the scene of the crime. How could she imagine her paintings would actually captivate anyone? Just who would find the clash of colors exciting or effective? She obviously did, but would anyone else? And the childish simplicity of her figures, trees, chairs—how could she not think that people wouldn't see how clumsy, amateurish, pretentious, and stupid they were. If Saada were in Beirut, Suha would have asked her advice. Saada would have helped her. He remembered what a French critic had told him about how inferior the art of today was, how shallow the artists were, and how ignorant they were of the more complicated techniques of their profession, avoiding the painstaking work which was the true mark of creation. Could he have said that of her? She had studied, toiled, labored for years before daring to exhibit her work. Then again, what was her public's expectations? Her public? She had studied for herself, toiled for herself, so why then would she care what the public thought?

As soon as she closed the door, the doorbell rang. Nadia! Thank God she was here. To hell with the paintings! Could the creation of an artist ever compare with the creation of a human being, her daughter, whom she had carried, given birth to, brought up? Others saw Nadia as she saw her: beautiful, intelligent, special. She had created life, not something inanimate. God had blessed her with the capability to have children, even if he hadn't given her the talent to paint.

"Hello dear."

She wanted the kiss to remove the anxiety and doubt, the fear of failure, or so she hoped.

"How was your day?"

She went into the kitchen to fix Nadia's lunch. She filled the jug, lit the stove. She put out two cups, two plates. Was there anyone at the exhibition yet? Had it attracted any interest? Were they talking about the artist?

"Would you like a piece of gâteau or baklava with your tea, dear?"

Suddenly Nadia burst out laughing and said, "Mama, you're not even listening to me! I just told you we celebrated Lamia's birthday at school, and the birthday cake was great. And now you're asking me what I want to eat!"

"Why not? You might be still hungry."

She felt herself blush in response to Nadia's laughter. Even her daughter found her unconvincing. How then could she expect to convince strangers of what she was trying to express in her paintings? She carried the cups of tea to the sitting room. She gave one to Nadia and sat down facing her. She sipped her tea while her daughter chatted to her, but she never heard a single word.

୬ଡ଼

Should she phone or go there? No sooner had Anwar left the apartment, shutting the door behind him, than she went up and stood in front of the telephone, unable to make up her mind. If she phoned, it would allay the unease, the embarrassment, the disappointment. And what if she had sold any? She wanted to see for herself the red "sold" dot on the painting, and hear people's comments as Samaan pointed to this painting or that. Her hand froze on the door handle. How conceited! It would be best to hear the truth over the telephone where she would be shielded from the gloating eyes.

She dialed the number and let it ring two, three times . . . five, six, seven. Why was no one picking up? Her wandering gaze fell on the clock in front of her; then she let out a nervous laugh. How could she have forgotten the club didn't open till ten!

She went back to her housework. If she moved the hands of the clock, would it be possible to move time forward? When nine o'clock came round, she couldn't wait any longer and got dressed. She gave Babu final instructions and hurried out into the road. She headed over to the shops and stores, passing one shop window after another, eyeing the dresses, shoes, household goods, watches, jewelry.

She looked at her watch—it was a half hour before it opened. She refused to stand outside like a beggar trying to get people to come in, so she went into a store to buy some shoes.

She walked through the club door at ten-fifteen, hugging the wall on the right-hand side, her eyes fixed on the floor. An ostrich! If she didn't see anyone, they wouldn't see her! She entered the exhibition hall.

Her heart was beating so, it deafened her, held her back. There were footsteps in the corridor outside, so she went up to one of the paintings. No red dot in the corner. Rage filled her. People bought paintings a lot worse than this! Samaan was right—they bought the name. People were stupid and shallow; they didn't know what art was; they had no idea. She lowered her eyes and moved on to the next. Not even a drunkard had been drunk enough to look at them. She refused to sell her name. She was exhibiting her art, not her name. Anwar would really enjoy this. And the people, the people she had snubbed because of her painting. Her painting! It was lucky she hadn't signed the paintings with her own name. She smiled sarcastically. Coward! That's what Saada would have called her if she'd been here. Saada! What would Saada think of her paintings if she saw them? Her eyes roamed over the rest of the paintings hanging on the wall in front of her. Was she really seeing what she was seeing, or was it just her imagination? Apprehensive yet hopeful, she forced herself on. Two paintings sold! Her heart pounded violently. She stood motionless before the paintings. Had any others been sold? Terrified of dashing her hopes, she wavered between curiosity and fear. Two paintings would only pay back a small part of what she owed. But getting his money back wasn't what he wanted. He only wanted her to enjoy herself! The insult had made her challenge fate, had made her pursue this course.

"Good morning, Suha!"

The voice brought her back sharply. She turned around to see Fadia Darweesh.

"You've come to see the paintings, too? Samer was at the club last night, and he told me there's no harm done for an unknown artist to exhibit her work. Have you looked at them? 'No harm done!' Really, he never told me they were so amateurish."

Before Suha could reply, the woman beside her chattered on, "I'm lucky you're here. You know something about art, and I need a painting for the sitting-room wall. I'd like you to help me choose one, if you will."

Suha was afraid her bright red face would give her away. Her coming here had been a mistake. Why hadn't it crossed her mind she might run into someone she knew? Her presence here was a lie, a deception.

"What do you think of that one? Oh, it's been sold."

Suha looked at the frame of the paintings in front of which Fadia and she were standing. A third painting! She got a hold of herself and cast an eye around the rest of the paintings.

"Let's see which ones haven't been sold yet," Suha said. "And I'll pick out the best one for you."

She laughed at herself. She was pretending to look at the paintings when in reality she was only looking at the frames, trying to see if there were a red dot. However, how could she make a choice between her creations, her children?

"What do you think of this one?"

Fadia stood there waiting for her opinion. Suha was silent for a while, then said, "The bare tree leaning over the chair. The chair is empty but for a shawl draped over its side. The wind plays with the shawl and plays among the branches hanging over it . . . The movement of the branches and shawl suggests the passing of time, and the bare branches absence, as does the shawl. There was a woman or girl on the chair. Then she left, disappeared. But absence is not the end of existence or death since the tree remains and will put out leaves. And the girl—she will come back to get her shawl."

Fadia listened to Suha's comments in silence, then said, "But I don't like the knot growing out of the tree trunk, nor the colors—the deep purple of the shawl and the dark blue of the sky. Then there's the blue tree trunk! Who's ever heard of a blue tree trunk?"

Suha wanted to say, "Van Gogh!" but she said, "Sure. But a tree owes its life to the sky, doesn't it? The tree trunk, therefore, reflects the color of the sky, only more intensely, and the brightly colored shawl is the first thing that grabs your attention. Mankind has always thought of itself as master of the universe and at the very center of it all, yet mankind itself is absent from the painting. It's as if the artist wants the universe to be the master, the universe and time."

The artist? Suha smiled. Only when she had stopped talking did Suha notice the strange expression in Fadia's eyes as she hung on her every word. Fadia's features stirred and she said, "You really must be an art expert, Suha. Did you have to look at the painting long to see all that?"

Had she fallen into the trap?

"Anyone who has a trained eye through studying art and has read critical studies of the most famous paintings can see what a modest amateur wants to express."

"That's true. I've never heard of her before. You've certainly made me want to buy something by her. Should I get this one?"

"If it's . . . a good painting, I would say yes."

And Fadia bought the painting.

৯৯

Nine years later, they returned to Beirut. The newspapers were full of news about Black September in Jordan. The months, too, had changed color.

While Anwar shaved, the voice from the transistor radio in the kitchen drifted in: "The French news agency in Jordan has reported that casualties of Wednesday's clashes between the Palestinians and the Jordanian army number twenty-three dead and one hundred sixty-nine injured. The agency obtained the number from an official in the Palestinian Red Crescent." He pressed the on button of the radio in front of him and turned up the sound of the classical music to drown out the voice in the kitchen.

He came back from the hospital that evening and was greeted by the voice of the radio announcer: "Since seven o'clock this morning, Amman began to prepare for another black day after the cease-fire agreed by the government and the fedayeen broke down yesterday . . . Carloads of fedayeen have been roaming the streets of Amman demanding that merchants close their stores." He went into the bathroom to wash his hands, but the voice followed him: "A short while afterwards, sporadic gun and artillery fire reverberated throughout the deserted city as people raced to their homes. Amman has once more become a ghost town . . ."

He put his fingers in his ears to stop the voice. It was like his house! Where was the Suha he loved? She had been unhappy in the Gulf, so he had let the house become filled with paper, canvas, wooden frames, the smell of oil paints, and he had said nothing. They stopped seeing most of the people they knew, and he had said nothing, waiting for them to return to Beirut so that she could go back to the life she knew, to her sister, the people she knew. And now?

He walked into the dining room to have breakfast and was greeted by the same voice: "The Palestinian Red Crescent has announced that civilian and fedayeen casualties from recent incidents number 150 dead and 500 injured." His temper boiled over. He reached out, pressed the button, and turned off the voice. Immediately Suha shouted out angrily, "They may not be your people, but aren't you concerned what's happening to them!"

He pressed the button: ". . . All that can be seen in the sky are tracer rounds and fires burning in the direction of the airport and elsewhere."

He took the coffee pot, filled his cup, and ate his breakfast in silence. Suha had let the coffee get cold.

"Has Nadia gone down to wait for the bus?"

Suha's eyes were glued to the needle on the transistor radio as though trying to make sense of what was being broadcast. Anwar looked closely at the pale face, the knot of concentration and worry between her eyebrows, the tightly pursed lips.

"Suha! Has Nadia gone down to wait for the school bus?" he said, raising his voice in anger.

"Yes!"

He didn't miss the angry tone in her curt reply. He finished his breakfast without uttering another word. He wondered whether to say good-bye to her. A smile once again danced on his lips. Did she even notice he was there for him to tell her he was going? He left, slamming the door behind him. Suha tuned the knob to the Cairo station, then turned up the volume so she could hear it as she went between the dining room and kitchen. The announcer was repeating the same old news, so she turned it down and went into her studio. He was only concerned about his patients! It was as if the people who had been wounded, maimed, or killed in Jordan weren't as human as his patients. Weren't her people his people? She lifted up the frame she had put the canvas on the day before, placed it on the easel, and fixed her attention on the brush pot—the wide brush was best; its strokes were bold and powerful. She wiped it with a towel, picked out a tube of paint, squeezed it, and a thread of blue flowed out onto the palette. She would paint, paint how the people lived, their homes, their churches and mosques, their weddings and celebrations. No one would wipe it out, wipe it out of existence. Her brush moved quickly and gracefully across the canvas.

9

Half-past four. In another hour they would bring her dinner. The doctor would come. She closed her eyes.

☜

"Saada, telephone!" Salma yelled from downstairs.

"Who is it?"

"I forgot to ask . . . A young man."

I heard giggling as I rushed downstairs. They were probably winking as well.

"Hello?"

"Saada?"

My heart jumped.

"It's Ali."

"I know, I recognized your voice."

"Why didn't you answer my letters?"

Maybe it was because I was scared he was another Amer, or maybe because he was "not like everyone else, different."

"Because I didn't have anything to tell you."

He should have called me a liar, but he said, "When can I see you?"

See you? Maybe I should have ended the relationship before it went any further? What about all our walks, all we shared, and all the conversations which made me forget my feelings of loss? The temptation was too strong to resist.

"Afternoon . . . Tomorrow?"

"This afternoon. See you then."

I put the phone down. Today was sooner than tomorrow. He had said, "This afternoon." I went back to my room. The book was still open on my desk. I sat down, running my eyes over the print. What should I say? I snapped the book shut and put it back on the shelf. I took a notebook—Andalusian literature—and opened it: Jadeed Ibn Shaheed—"Of Conformists and Innovators." The word for "innovators" in Arabic also means "storms," which reminded me of the inner storms I was experiencing . . . But what did I have to lose? I wasn't a child anymore. I wasn't going to repeat the experience with Amer. I had learned my lesson. But what, though? That I wasn't thinking about Ali when I was talking about the film Fadia and I had seen? That I wasn't weighing Ali and Baha's opinions when Ali had criticized the performance of some musician we had seen recently? That I wasn't thinking about Ali, comparing him with my other male friends? Let him, they were all my friends. He was a friend like all the rest . . . I left Ibn Shaheed with his conformists and his innovators to try and persuade Sumayya to go with me to the souk.

৯৯

I stood before the mirror, buttoning my silk blouse. I then stepped into my charcoal skirt, hitched it up to my waist, and started to turn it around, adjusting it until it felt comfortable. I reached out for my red lipstick.

"Who are you getting all dressed-up for?"

I didn't reply, only bending down to tie the laces on my sandals.

"Is Ali back?"

My face turned bright red and I snapped back, "It's none of your business! Anyway, aren't I always concerned with my appearance?"

Sumayya went quiet for a while. I could feel her eyes following my every movement. She then said, "You've really changed, Saada. In the year I've known you, you've lost a lot of weight."

I stood in front of the mirror again, smoothing the creases in my skirt.

"My schoolmates used to make fun of me: 'Saada the monkey, she hops around the pantry.'" I smiled, then continued: "I can laugh about it now, but I didn't laugh about it then. I hated my name and I hated myself."

"Did you decide there was no point in caring what you looked like?"

"Totally, Sumayya. But Egypt changed me."

She looked me up and down for a while; then she said in a hushed tone, "You do look different. But how about your attitude?"

Her question stung me. What was she trying to imply? I retorted, "Doesn't the way you look affect the way you think and the way you think affect the way you look?"

"Please, don't try applying psychological theories to me," she said sarcastically. "Leave that to the professors."

How I would laugh at myself a couple of years later when I recalled what she had said.

⁂

He was waiting for me outside the entrance to Casino Biba. Even from a distance I could make out his slender frame, the white light-weight shirt and gray pants, his shiny black hair. I quickened my pace.

When he saw me, a smile spread across his face from ear to ear.

"Hi there . . . I missed you!"

He reached out and clasped my hand and squeezed. The warmth of his hands flowed into my body, setting it on fire. I told myself over and over, "He's a friend," as I tried to control my feelings.

"How was your vacation?" I said.

"Didn't you get my letters?"

My face turned red. My tongue tripped. Stupid girl! I didn't even know how to start a conversation with him.

"Of course I did. They told me about what you did, who you saw . . . It looks like you had a great time."

I laughed to cover up how awkward I felt. By then we were in the Casino Biba grounds, so he led me to a table in a corner away from the street.

"If you had been there with me, it would have made my vacation."

Did he really mean that or was he just being polite? However I couldn't stop my heart from racing. I changed the topic, saying, "Cairo in summer is really boring. All my friends went away, back to their hometowns or Alexandria. Baha was the only one who stayed here, so I used to get together with him from time to time."

It was Atayet, not Baha, but I wanted to see how he would react, what he would say, and to stir up his jealousy. I was watching his every expression. But then he said quietly, "So, I believe you couldn't find anything to write to me about?"

"Believe what you like," I snapped back.

However, the puzzled look in his eyes gave me certain satisfaction.

⁂

We were cramming. I would stay behind in the library to study a journal or a reference book, and would return in the evening with an armful of books. I spent half the night reading, studying lecture notes. Between notes and textbook, and subject to subject, Ali would spring to mind. I would open a book, and his image would form over the print. I'd go over in my mind our last date, what he had said, the tone of his voice, the expression on his face, the way he laughed. Minutes would go by; then I would jerk my thoughts out of my memories and go back to my notes or the book in front of me. When Thursday came around, I became even more distracted and less able to wrest my thoughts from the past. I went back to the dorm at noon and stayed there, waiting for him to call, to go for a walk, or do something fun he had suggested for the weekend. He would call in the evening, and sometimes he wouldn't. Sumayya noticed my restlessness and my agitation, and said, "Hasn't Ali called?"

I erupted, replying sarcastically, "Why, did he tell you he was going to call?"

She became quiet, and her face flushed red with embarrassment. I tried to smooth things out, saying, "Why should he call me? If he thought it necessary, he would have done so. He has a lot of studying to do in his final year."

In that way, I tried to calm my nerves, to reassure myself, but it was no use. Couldn't he just talk to me without us going out somewhere. Didn't he know I had anticipated he would need some weekends free to catch up on his studies? Could he do without me so easily? And me? I hit the books, too, to keep myself busy so I wouldn't keep searching for the answers to my questions. I opened the *Diwan* of Abu Nuwas, and my eyes fell on the line: "How can one who is touched by desire and longing be at peace?"

I smiled wryly to myself. Wasn't the reason I loved literature because it mirrored my inner self? Was I now deluded in thinking that it would distract me from that inner self? I closed the *Diwan* of Abu Nuwas.

Days went by, and with them the pain of disappointment faded little by little to be replaced anew by the anxiety of waiting, waiting for the phone to ring on Thursday evening. Two or three weeks passed without my hearing his voice. I'd arrange with Sumayya or Atayet to see a film, any film they chose, just so that I could tell him I was busy when he phoned and couldn't go out with him that Friday. Furious, I'd watch the film with Sumayya or Atayet. I'd watch it but not see a thing; then I'd go back to more studying and more waiting.

One day the dorm maid called up, "Sitt Saada, telephone!"

I jumped up from my seat and hurried to pick up the phone. Should I snub him?

"Hello, Saada? It's Ali."

It was as if I hadn't been waiting to hear from him all those three weeks!

"How are you?" I asked him, putting on a Lebanese accent.

I hid all the desire, disappointment, blame as I heard him softly say, "What are you doing tomorrow? A friend of mine has given me two tickets to *Rigoletto* at the opera. Are you interested in going?"

And he, did he really want me to go along, or did he not want the ticket to go to waste? What about the date I had made with Atayet to go buy some shoes I needed? The temptation was too strong to resist.

"Of course I'm interested. You know very well my budget doesn't stretch to the opera."

When I met him at three the next day, he held out two white carnations, and said with a smile, "I didn't forget it's your favorite flower."

My temper vanished, and I forgot I had decided to affect an air of coolness and indifference. My heart was racing, only because I loved carnations, of course.

The following week we watched the film *Intermezzo*, and afterwards we strolled along the bank of the Nile, talking and discussing as usual. As usual, I waited for him to call on Thursday evening. The call never came. Two more weeks went by, and I still didn't hear from him. He had to be studying, or it was the chilly Cairo nights. Should he leave his room to phone me from a shop? To say what? That he's studying? The memory of the two carnations healed the pain and disappointment, and it also made me forget the disappointment of the day we spent at Maadi. And in the end I gave in to a reality I didn't dare try to see clearly. He had cut himself off from me for weeks on end only to come back to me, and I never once asked him the reason why. My dignity, my shyness maybe? But he came back to me as though nothing had happened, came back with his gentle, affectionate manner, his attentiveness which banished whatever anxiety, doubt, and fear I was feeling. Maybe they had been banished by my fantasy, the fantasy I wanted to become a reality. I only realized this when Sumayya, my roommate, who kept vigil over my movements and periods of silence, or rather my thoughts and feelings, asked me, "Why do you wait for him? If he were serious about you, he wouldn't snub you for weeks at a time!"

The accusation stung my dignity. Had she guessed how worried I was? Could she read the apprehension in my face? Putting on a calm air, I replied, "He's not snubbing me. I just don't want to interrupt his studying."

"If you just made a short phone call, it wouldn't interrupt him. In fact, it would help him study!"

I shot back furiously, "Don't patronize me just because you don't have a boyfriend!"

"The reason I'm not dating anyone is that I can do without a boyfriend like him," she replied nonchalantly.

I was so mad—angry, embarrassed, and insulted—I couldn't speak. Had I somehow betrayed my feelings without realizing? How did Sumayya know when I hadn't told anyone? Was it because I had broken a date with her or Atayet any time Ali happened to call? Or was it the carnations I had brought back from time to time, only throwing them out after they had all wilted? Her voice cut through the fog of my agitation: "Saada, you are dearer to me than a sister, but love isn't just when a young man takes an interest in you, takes you out for a walk, takes you to a party or . . ."

"Who said I was in love! He's just a friend like all the rest of the boys I know."

"Sure, that's why you stopped seeing all your other friends."

Her sarcasm wounded me, but she walked out of the room before I could say anything in reply.

ॐ

"Sitt Saada, Sitt Saada!"

She felt the hand gently touching hers before the nurse's soft voice registered. She opened her eyes.

"Your dinner's here. Can you eat it by yourself or do you need help?"

The nurse turned the crank and raised the upper half of the bed; then she took the cover off one of the dishes.

"What else is there besides soup?"

The nurse took the cover off the other dish: "A chicken leg and mashed potatoes."

She put back the cover and placed the napkin under the patient's chin. Next she took hold of the spoon, dipped it into the soup and brought it up to Saada's mouth.

"I'll feed you the soup before it gets cold. I'll take the skin off the chicken. Then you can do the rest."

A sickly smile spread across the face of the patient.

"Don't bother, I'm still strong enough to take the skin off a chicken leg."

The nurse smiled in response: "I'd prefer you to use your own hands as well. That way you can exercise your muscles."

"Don't I use them when I get out of bed and go to the bathroom?"

"On your hands?"

The patient laughed.

"Splendid! I see that Sitt Saada has started to laugh again!"

Only then did the two women notice the doctor standing by the door. The nurse leaned toward him and asked, "Do you want to examine her, doctor?"

"No, I don't want to interrupt her dinner."

However he went up to the bed, took hold of her wrist and felt her pulse as he looked at his watch. After a minute he said, "Excellent. Pulse regular. And you're taking food. I want you to try sleeping at night without a sedative. I'll come by tomorrow morning to take a look at the incision."

"What do the tests say, doctor. Have you got the results yet?"

Grinning broadly, he replied, "I ask myself if I actually need to examine you. You seem perfectly alert. Yes, Sitt Saada, the tests have come back. There's no need to worry."

Saada never once took her eyes off the doctor's face, studying every expression and gesture he made.

"When can I go home," she asked joyfully.

"Only when we're sure your temperature is not going to go up again and there's no infection. You'll have to come back a week later so I can examine you. Then we'll take your stitches out."

He caressed her hand: "You're going to be fine."

He left the room, followed by the nurse. Saada went back to her dinner, eating slowly.

She tossed and turned in her bed. He told her not to take sleeping pills—that was a good sign. But what if the incision started to give her pain? The point was that she was getting better. She was going to go home, back to her students. Her eyes fell on the bouquet of carnations, and she turned out the light.

He was my one love, my true love. A one-sided love maybe? But what about the letters he wrote? Was I wrong in thinking they were love letters? His letters didn't stop coming for a whole year, except for last month. Letters from the Ali I knew, who understood me, made me happy, the Ali I liked, loved. I never thought of asking myself, "Does he love me." Just one kiss—the kiss good-bye. It set me on fire. He only kissed me that one time? Probably because he respected me. He enjoyed talking with me; he found me interesting; he understood me. If I had understood him, there would have been no disappointment, no hurt.

৯

"Finally, I'm done with college."

I kissed Mama and Suha, who were waiting for me at the airport. "Let's go home."

Mama gave the taxi driver the address—a street I had never heard of. I had never seen the house. What did it look like, this strange house? Our house was in Jerusalem. Papa was in Jerusalem. But Ali was here. When would I see him?

"Saada, what are you thinking about?" Suha said, managing to get my attention. "I want to know what your plans are. I told you a while back how I was doing at the bank. I got promoted a week ago and now . . ."

"Suha," Mama interrupted. "Saada is tired, let her rest before you ask her what her plans are. In any case, she doesn't know Beirut."

Actually I did. I knew it from what Ali had told me, seen it through Ali's eyes. But I didn't tell her that.

"Suha's right, Mama," I said. "It's time I got a job and paid my way." Suha's face grew red.

"I never meant that!" Suha replied.

"I know you didn't, but don't think me so self-centered."

I was thinking about Ali above all else, and there I was claiming I wasn't self-centered! But I didn't feel ashamed. Mama and Suha didn't know Ali, didn't even know of his existence.

"Why are you smiling?"

"Because I'm here with both of you, and I'm happy," I lied.

I drew Suha to me and said, "I missed you, you misfortunate thing. I got used to having you around!"

I wasn't lying.

                        🙟

The first thing on my mind was to phone Ali.

"Ali? He's not home. Who's calling?"

Despite my disappointment, I replied calmly, "A friend from Cairo."

"And your name?"

I ignored her question and gave her my phone number.

"I'll be in this evening if he wants to call back."

The evening turned to night, and he didn't phone. She must not have given him the number. If it was the servant, she probably forgot. If it was his mother or sister—the proverbial jealous rivalry of the mother-in-law and her daughter-in-law, and I smiled. But I wasn't a wife or even a fiancée. Who would know? For love's sake I called him up again.

"He's not home. Who's calling?"

I replied to the question with another question: "Didn't you give him my phone number?"

"Ah, you're the friend from Cairo. He came in late last night, but I gave him your number."

I waited impatiently for evening to come. I turned down going with Mama and Suha to my aunt's, pretending to be tired and weary. Whenever the phone rang, I jumped up to answer it. Eventually, it was him.

"Saada? Thank God you got here safe and sound! When did you get here?"

"The day before yesterday."

I forgot I had intended to hide my longing and keep up a pretense of indifference in reply to his own indifference since I was going to pretend I had been here a week or two, but his sweet voice on the other end of the line made me forget everything.

"I'd like to . . ."

See you?

". . . introduce you to my fiancée."

My ears were filled with a ringing which struck me deaf, dumb, and blind. The room began to swirl around me, so I sat down.

"Hello, hello? Saada?"

His voice seemed to be coming from another planet.

"Hello?"

I hung up and just sat there, unable to move, for several minutes, maybe more. The telephone rang and rang. I didn't reach out to pick it up, I just sat there. Eventually, it stopped ringing.

His fiancée? Was that why he had stopped writing recently? Stupid girl! Amer and now Ali! Why did I ever think he loved me? Because he showed interest in me, invited me to go out with him, had fun with me? Just like Amer. I thought he was "different, not like everyone else." He never once said he loved me. He said he was a friend. Why didn't I believe him? What about the feeling of warmth that flowed into my body? Just mine, not his. Sumayya was right—had it ever been love? His fiancée, she was probably rich and beautiful, unlike me, Saada the monkey. Nobody loved me. They had fun with me, yes, listened to my chatter and jokes, even. And me? Saada the monkey. He was just interested in me as a friend, so I fell in love with him. I fussed about what to wear, how to do my hair, putting on makeup. Stupid girl! I was still Saada the monkey, and nobody would ever love me. Was it because of who I was, because of love and them, my love, the poetry of love? Art? What an artist imagined or created? I got up to wash my face to try and bring myself back to life.

When the rays from the sun made their way into the room through the gaps in the curtains, Saada Rayyis was in a deep sleep.

10

There was a gentle knock on the door.

"Yes?"

The nurse opened the door and came in.

"I thought you might be asleep. There are two visitors for you in reception. Should I let them in?"

"Who are they?"

"I didn't ask. I didn't know if you were asleep or not."

She walked up to the bed, raised the upper half, then arranged the pillows behind the patient's back. She repeated the question: "Should I let them in?"

"Sure."

Who could they be? Haifa knew Suha and Anwar. My students? She looked toward the door when she sensed movement outside. It couldn't be! The smile froze on her lips.

The man took hold of the woman's arm, and they walked up to the bed.

"Saada, this is my wife Najwa. You're getting to meet her at last."

I never thought I'd be introduced to her or see him. She reached out to shake hands.

"Pleased to meet you. Please, sit down."

I pointed to the two chairs near the bed. She was plain, but dressed elegantly. So, he must have married her for her money.

"How did you know I was in the hospital?"

He hadn't changed except for the gray at his temples.

"My niece is a student of yours," his wife replied.

"Your niece?"

"Rana Shaaban."

"Why did she never mention that she . . . that . . . Ali was her aunt's husband?"

Fifteen years! I thought he had totally vanished from my life.

৯৯

"Saada, phone!" Mama called out.

"Who is it?"

"I didn't ask."

I raised the receiver to my ear.

"Hello?"

"Saada?"

What did he want—to introduce me to his fiancée? Good luck to him! "Yes," I replied in a flat tone, then said nothing more.

"When I got cut off a couple of days ago, I tried to call you again. The phone rang, but no one answered so I thought it was out of order."

I didn't say anything, so he continued: "When can I see you? I want to . . ."

"Introduce me to your fiancée? Congratulations!"

Could he tell I was angry? So let him! Only he said quite calmly, "You're sure to like Najwa. When can we meet?"

I replied abruptly, "I'm very busy these days. I'm looking for a job, and I don't want to tie myself down by making a commitment."

"Even in the evening?"

"In the evening I'll be tired. I go to bed early."

He paused for a moment, then said, "Okay, fine. I wish you every success . . . I'll call you some other time."

Two weeks later, he called me again.

"How's the job search going?"

"I got a position teaching in high school. I'm going to teach Arabic literature to seniors."

"Congratulations! . . . So, can we see you now?"

How could I get rid of him? Didn't he get the message or have any idea?

"When?"

"Whenever you like . . . Tomorrow evening?"

"I'm sorry," I replied without a moment's thought, "But I promised my mother I'd go see a film with her tomorrow."

"The day after, then?"

"My aunt's invited us for dinner."

He was quiet for a while, then said, "It looks like you're really busy. Give me a call when you have a moment to spare."

I didn't miss the flatness in his voice. He had gotten the message at last. I wasn't a doll he could play with then toss aside when he had had enough. I never called him. My eyes would fall on the telephone. Should I speak to him? But what was the use? He had someone else. I waited for the wound to heal . . .

Once I saw him walking twenty yards ahead, of me so I quickened my pace toward him. A chance meeting wasn't the same as calling him on the phone. He crossed the road. I crossed over to the other side as well. Then he looked behind him. I stood rooted to the spot. How strange it was . . .

One time I sat in the movie theater, watching the people as they came in. How could he possibly miss a really good movie like this? The lights went down. The show began. Why would he want to go and see a film these days anyway? Stupid girl! I couldn't make sense of what the actors were saying, and minutes later I left the theater . . .

In the Café de Paris, Suha was telling me about her colleague Salah's engagement party. I wasn't really listening to her—I was too busy looking over at the sidewalk outside. It was a waste of time. He didn't walk past.

Only years later did the wound heal. But it left a scar.

❧

The memory taunted her, but it vanished when Najwa remarked, "You know what young men and women are like at that age—'Miss will think I'm trying to suck up to her for a good grade.'"

For the first time he opened his mouth and said, "Is it a good or a bad grade you're going to give her?"

He had lost none of his quick-wittedness. He smiled, "What do you think?"

Once again his wife spoke up: "Sitt Saada, the point is that you inspired in your students a love of the Arabic language and Arabic literature."

"I don't deserve the credit for that. The credit goes to Arabic literature itself. What could be more beautiful than our poetry?"

Ali looked at his wife: "When I first got to know Saada at college, I thought it strange a Christian could love the Arabic language so much and study it as a major."

Saada stared at him in disbelief. *Since when does my religion matter in his perception of me?* No, he had changed. She blurted out, "Ali! What has religion got to do with language? Are you saying that it has?"

His wife added, "Have you forgotten all the Christian bellettrists and poets? Pre-Islam? Just look who's behind the literary renaissance in Lebanon and the Arab press in Egypt. Sitt Saada is right!"

It shocked her how much her friend had changed. Or was she wrong about that, too? She changed the topic.

"Please, don't say *Sitt,* just call me Saada. So, tell me about you two?"

Ali said nothing. Was he annoyed? But Najwa spoke up: "We have two girls and a boy. Lena, our eldest, is thirteen, and our youngest, Bilal, is seven. And they're all doing well at school, praise be to God."

"That's good . . . But what about you?"

Najwa fell silent. She seemed to hesitate. A minute went by, then she said, "I used to be a teacher before I was married. Like you, I taught Arabic language and literature. However, Ali wanted me to give up work after we got married . . . But I'm kept busy with the children."

It flashed through her mind: *he married Najwa because she was like me.* Stupid woman! You can keep on deluding yourself—she was the same religion as him! She wanted to say, "Was he worth it?" to console Najwa about the profession she gave up, but she said, "I love teaching because I love children. I don't have any children . . . My students are my children."

"I myself loved teaching for a different reason. I think you understand, Saada, that you are never happier when you feel you are imparting knowledge, even it's only in some small way, and that you're creating a desire for knowledge."

Ali butted in: "What a load of nonsense! Every child has a desire for knowledge. Look at how curious our own children are, Najwa, and their endless questions. Don't give your profession or any other profession more credit than it deserves."

Was he justifying why he had prevented his wife from working? Was he putting her down, ridiculing her ideals?

"There might be some exaggeration in what Najwa is saying, but you cannot deny that one characteristic of teaching is that we interact with people at the critical stages of their lives—in elementary school with all that childhood innocence, in high school with young teenage boys and girls, where the reality of society and life's frustrations have yet to rob them of their hopes and ideals."

He didn't hide his sarcasm when he replied, "'Childhood innocence!' I think you're the one who's being naive, Saada, laboring under such illusions. It would seem that age and experience haven't robbed you of your ideals and faith in mankind, and . . ."

"On the contrary, I lost them a long time ago!"

She wanted to add "Because of you," but didn't, and said, "It's because young people do have hopes and ideals, I can awaken and foster in them a love of what these hopes and ideals are trying to express."

She paused, then smiled and continued: "Have you forgotten your own love for poetry?"

"Excuse me!" The nurse was standing at the door.

"The doctor isn't allowing long visits yet. I'm sorry, but I'll have to ask you to leave our patient now."

"Of course, of course."

Ali promptly complied and stood up. Maybe he was grateful that such an awkward visit had come to an end. But then, why had he come? Najwa held out her hand to shake farewell: "We hope you have a speedy recovery, Saada. We'll see you soon, God willing. You won't manage to give us the slip again."

She laughed when she said that; then they left.

Why did he come? And why did he send flowers? Like me she is a teacher of Arabic language and literature. Like me she is neither rich nor beautiful. But unlike me she isn't a Christian. The difference in religion doesn't stop us becoming friends, doesn't stop us having tastes or opinions in common. Ali never once made me feel religion was an obstacle between us. Never? Or at least I never felt it was? I never felt it strange a Christian should love the Arabic language. I didn't realize that religion might prevent love or marriage . . . Naive and idealistic. Ali is right. How he has changed! Or perhaps he hasn't.

Feeling weary, she closed her eyes.

୬

Morocco! I'd heard about it and read about it, and I was there at last. I had traveled to certain unique cities, drawn by the spirit of their past—architecture, history, and religious importance. Jerusalem, my birthplace, Istanbul, Venice, Rome—their stones spoke to me of their eternity. And now, Fez. I stood gazing at the large stone basins in which the tanners immersed their hides, but the radiant colors couldn't mask the revolting, choking smell. However, I forgot about it as soon as I entered the Madrasat Attarine. I gazed in awe at the colorful mosaics which covered its walls and columns as I stood under a ceiling of intricately carved cedar—the art and architecture of the Marinids at their zenith. A profound silence enveloped the place, rising from a bygone magnificence, from a holy past. The mosque of Qaraouiyine? No tourists allowed. I would have to visit another less important, less famous mosque. So, from Fez to Marrakesh, to La Fna square with its vendors and jugglers and clowns, and onto the Kutubiyya mosque, which I was just about to enter when, "No, no!! No Europeans!"

The curator of the mosque stood right in my face, blocking my way. Me, European?

"No, I'm Arab, from Lebanon!"

He immediately drew back, and a wide smile took the place of the threatening scowl, then he placed his hand on his chest and bowed in welcome.

"Welcome Muslim sister from Lebanon, welcome, please go in."

Was it because the Moroccans were all Muslims they didn't know there were Christian Arabs as well? Of course, I didn't tell him anything. I took off my shoes and went into the mosque.

৵

A Belgian engineer asked me, "Is it possible to have two brothers where one is Muslim and the other Christian?"

I found his question quite strange. I thought for a moment and replied, "Only if one of them converts to a religion he wasn't born into. But that's rare."

"I didn't mean that. Is it possible one of them can be born a Christian and the other a Muslim?"

I didn't understand. Was it possible the Belgian was born a Catholic and his brother a Protestant? So I asked him. He explained, "I know three Lebanese brothers. One of them is called Marwan, and the other two, Pierre and Antoine."

I laughed and laughed in his puzzled face.

"Just because he has an Arab name he must be Muslim?"

A refined-looking Belgian woman entered the conversation: "What are the Arabs? Aren't they Muslims?"

If this was what well-educated people were thinking, what could I expect from the rest?

Irritated, I replied, "Most of the Arabs are Muslims, but there are Christian Arabs as well. For example, I'm a Christian Arab."

"A Christian Arab? I've never heard of that before."

I tried to explain.

"Some Arabs were Christian or Jewish before the coming of Islam, and a great number of the companions of the Prophet were Christians who helped him . . ."

I stopped talking since the faces that were turned away told me I was speaking about something which didn't interest anyone. How could anyone in the world be interested in trivia!

Saada, wrapped in her coat, was sitting on a chair in the hospital room, waiting for Suha and Anwar. She looked at her watch —eleven o'clock and they still hadn't come. She glanced over at the window. Maybe the heavy rain was holding them up, as it usually did. Her eyes fell on the bed which had been stripped of its sheets. Two weeks were like two months and she had to stay at home for two more weeks. After that came the end of semester and the vacation. And what about her students? The doctor hadn't paid that question any attention when she had asked him. All he was concerned about was her incision.

ॐ

"Miss, when are you coming back?"

The hope in their eyes revived her. Her students missed her.

"I'm leaving hospital tomorrow, but I have to rest for two weeks before I can go back to work."

Sameer burst out, "But the curriculum, Miss? How can we complete it?"

Sameer was intelligent, successful . . . self-centered.

"But Yusef Janaab has taken over from me."

He fell silent. Nahaad hesitated then said, "He's not like you. He's all over the place."

And Hina said, "He doesn't go into any depth. He doesn't go over the text with us in detail like you did."

Beneath her annoyance was a hidden feeling of pride, but she said, "All teachers have their own way of doing things. It won't do you any harm to get to know different approaches . . ."

"Different approaches?" Sameer interrupted excitedly. Then he got control of himself and said, "All he does is repeat everything from the book! We don't need him at all."

Was she worried or proud? About what, though? That they liked her? Ali had said, "You're the naive one. The years haven't robbed you of your ideals and faith in mankind." They were only looking out for themselves. Teenagers only liked doing something if there were something in it for them.

"We're sorry we're late, Saada."

Suha's voice returned her to the present as she and Anwar walked in.

"Anwar parked the car while I paid the bill. Can you imagine, it took a whole hour before we got to the cashier."

"I thought the rain had held you up."

Suha helped her to her feet while Anwar held her other arm.

"Does the scar from the surgery give you any pain?"

"Only slightly."

They walked slowly to the elevator.

৵

Suha put her cup of coffee down. Without looking at her sister she said, "I didn't want to bother you while you were in the hospital, Saada, but now you have to know."

"Know what?"

Has the doctor discovered something he's kept from me? Will I never go back to my students? Will I end up in agony like Mama? Suha noticed the signs of dismay on her sister's face, so she hurriedly replied, "Don't worry . . . It's just that we're going away."

"Again?"

"For the last time, God willing."

Saada didn't understand.

"For the last time? What do you mean?"

"I'm never coming back to this country. Even Anwar was convinced in the end. We're going to his brother's in Canada."

The surprise left her at a loss for words. Was she going to lose her sister again? Forever? She would never see her after today? What had happened? She tried to control her agitation as she asked Suha, "Do doctors earn more in Canada?"

Suha replied, a bitter smile on her lips, "He can't practice medicine there, Canada won't recognize his qualifications. In any case, it's no longer possible for him to practice here either."

The sisters fell silent. Then Saada asked, "What then?"

"He's going to look for a job, in administration or business, with a company which deals with hospitals, medical supplies."

Saada just looked at her sister, dumbfounded. Anwar, whose patients were the center of his life. She couldn't believe it!

Saada asked, "He would prefer to work in administration or business rather than in his profession?. . . What about your art, Suha! People have started to get to know you here and appreciate your paintings."

Suha replied proudly, "I started off here as an unknown artist, and I succeeded. I can make a fresh start there and succeed as well."

Saada wanted to tell her it was extremely competitive in the West, that it was bad enough for foreigners let alone Arabs to break into the jealous and closed world of art, but she asked her, "Does an artist remain an artist if torn from her roots?"

Suha shot back abruptly, "My roots! I don't have any roots here. You have roots, maybe, but I don't know why!"

Suha paused, then continued: "Even Anwar's a stranger in his own land. The war left him without any law to protect him, took away the government which upheld the law. Look around you! Who's looking out for us? Armed thugs, that's who!"

Saada looked at her dejectedly. *Suha, so this is the reason for your leaving.* She said bitterly, "It's true politics corrupts everything it touches."

Suha replied sharply, "If you mean my life, it was corrupted a long time ago. And politics played no part in that."

But Saada thought to herself: *Politics does play a part. And if not, then what is the reason for your sudden interest in politics? I was condemned for taking an interest in politics, criticized for taking part in demonstrations, for my hatred of foreigners, for showing bias toward my people. But was it toward my people or to my language and culture? Is bias intransigence? Suha is stuck in the past. Intransigence or loyalty? What's the use of intransigent loyalty or loyal intransigence?* She smiled: *Language once again. Or am I defending the chameleon which changed color whenever it changed country? Color, not blood. Blood flows, changes, gives life . . . It isn't intransigent, intransigence is death.*

"But politics only made things worse," Saada said to her sister. "Don't make Anwar the scapegoat."

Suha replied, clearly perturbed, "The Lebanese war made him a scapegoat. And he made me a scapegoat a long time ago, sacrificed to his work and his patients."

She choked on the last word. Saada noticed tears streaming in silence from her sister's eyes, so she said in an attempt to cheer her up, "But he loves you!"

"He loves me?"

Suha let out a strained, sarcastic laugh. *If Saada thinks this is love, then she really doesn't know what love is. Is she again trying to convince me or is she trying to silence her nagging conscience? Doesn't she notice Anwar has changed? That my relationship with him has changed?* Saada's voice penetrated her thoughts.

"Yes, he loves you! He works night and day to provide you and Nadia with every comfort and luxury."

Suha again exploded: "He lives night and day in his world where he works night and day! No conversation. No concern. No emotion. Is love . . ."

"Suha!" Saada cried out disapprovingly.

But Suha continued: "Is love buying us a color television, a bigger fridge, a new car? Buying, supplying, earning . . . A love valued at tens of thousands of liras, and not one penny of affection or concern. Love at a price!"

Suha choked on her humiliation. Love to Saada was always weighed and valued: Mounir—his qualifications, position, income. And she had let Saada persuade her. What did Saada know about love? She read about it in literature, in books. Love! She only loved herself! Then she heard Saada say, "'Pettiness begets bickering' as the proverb says . . ."

"Always so idealistic! You live in the world of literature, not of life. It's not apathy or indifference that causes people to bicker, is it?"

Could she believe what she was hearing? Saada said disapprovingly, "Suha, are you serious about what you're saying?"

Saada stopped for a moment, then said, "Have you forgotten how much in common you and Anwar have, and how much love and understanding there is between you?" She was met with a look of hatred in Suha's eyes.

"Love? Desire. Instinct. Or if it is love, then it has faded . . . It's gone."

Suha stopped talking, unable to hold back the tears any longer.

❧

Anwar took off his outer layer of clothing, put on the white surgical gown and pants, and went into the operating theater, throwing a quick glance at the anesthetized patient on the operating table. He washed his hands and put on the surgical gloves Samiya was holding out for him; then he bent down slightly so that she could tie the surgical mask around his nose and mouth. Samiya began sterilizing the skin around the stomach and waist while he looked among the instruments for a suitable scalpel. He leaned over the body stretched out in front of him, his fingers probing to determine where to make the incision. His hand froze. He heard a commotion outside; then the door behind him flew open, and something hard was thrust between his shoulder blades. A harsh voice said, "Stop what you're doing and take the bullet out of the comrade."

Before Anwar could take in what was happening, two armed men had pushed the operating table away from him, while some others had dragged in a table on which lay a young man covered in blood.

"Get a move on! Didn't you hear! Our comrade has a bullet in his chest. Take it out!"

The hard object was pressed into his back even harder. Then he heard his colleague Saad shout out behind him, "Are you crazy? Get out of here right now!"

A rifle was cocked, and an insolent voice replied, "We're not leaving. And if the doctor doesn't perform the operation immediately, we'll kill him!"

Was it a nightmare or reality? Anwar found himself surrounded on all sides—camouflage uniforms, rifles aimed at him. He didn't dare look at their faces. Through the heavy atmosphere of terror came Samiya's soft voice: "Get out. We'll operate on him. But we have to remove his clothing and sterilize . . ."

"Let him get started, then we'll leave," the insolent voice said.

Anwar moved his hands and used the scalpel to cut away the shirt from around the clumps of mud and coagulated blood. When the nurse took it off, the blood started to pour out.

"Stethoscope!"

Samiya quickly got it for him, and the armed men began to leave. The wounded man's heart was still beating, but it was faint and irregular. His body was convulsing and his hands were trembling. What if he died under the scalpel? And what if he didn't operate on him? The ache between his shoulder blades ended his speculation. Samiya began to disinfect the man's chest while Anwar turned around to get some sterilized forceps. He smiled as his eyes fell on the anesthetized patient who would regain consciousness before he had finished with the wounded man. He wanted to laugh, cry. Then he inserted the scalpel and forceps into the young man's chest.

❧

He headed over to the door to get rid of the clothes clinging to his body—the sweat of labor, concentration, fear. His hands closed around the door handle. No doubt they were waiting for him. He opened the door.

"Yes, Doctor?"

Six armed men were blocking the corridor, and behind them were two women, one old, one young. His heart started to beat rapidly.

"Did you take out the bullet?"

"Yes, thank God."

And thank God their question hadn't made him lie. But there was only one thing left to do. They moved aside to let him pass; then they burst into the operating theater. He dashed over to the stairway and ran down the steps. They wouldn't understand the bullet had damaged the heart, torn up an artery. There was nothing he could do, not him nor anyone. He entered his office, grabbed his case, and rushed out, since he could hear shrieking and shouting. He started the car and drove off.

He returned the concierge's greeting . . . For the last time, he told himself with a mixture of determination and despair.

❧

Saada sat, as usual, on the balcony, sipping her coffee and gazing at the sea. The sun had started to set, coloring the sky with red lines interspersed with long gray clouds. The lines stretched on and on, fading slowly whenever a cloud moved across. The sea was calm. She looked out, and all she could see was a slatelike flatness as far as the horizon. Glimmering on its surface here and there, flecks of white edged closer and closer. As they moved across the surface of the sea, they turned into ripples—wide, wide ripples which gathered momentum as they came nearer, rising and rolling, their crests crowned with glittering silver before crashing onto the shore in a creamy foam, then receding, their force spent, leaving on the sand their wet footprints.

She watched the movement of the waves, rolling, crashing, gathering. Their monotonous voice soothed and relaxed her nerves.

Politics had finally succeeded in taking Suha away from her . . . The war, not politics!

❧

"If it weren't for the Palestinians, the war in Lebanon would never have started."

"Don't they have the right to live like everyone else?" Suha replied.

"As long as they live like everyone else, yes. Not above everyone else, above the law. As long as they don't try to take over a country which isn't theirs."

"That's the fault of whoever let them!" Suha replied sarcastically.

I retorted angrily, "So, are you blaming whoever fought against them in Jordan? The Cairo Accord let them get away with what wouldn't be allowed in any other country. If only they had kept to it! Did we pay the price for our humanitarianism?"

"We? You, not I! I'm Palestinian!"

The Frenchman from next door butted in with a strange question: "Aren't you two sisters? How come only one of you is Palestinian?"

Suha rushed to respond, saying, "We're both Palestinian, but Saada is like a chameleon. She changes her allegiances whenever she changes countries."

"Or rather," I retorted, "Saada is loyal to the country she lives in. It took her in. She loves its people, its land. She's fair-minded, she doesn't think it's right that a people should take over a country which isn't theirs."

Suha came back with the familiar response: "But someone else has taken over their country!"

My own response was just as familiar: "So let them take revenge on whoever has taken over their country, not on the people who have let them into their country!"

The neighbor butted in again: "Both of you are right, but what..."

"It's easy for you to say who's right if it's not your country that's being threatened!" I said angrily. "And we don't expect somebody who has settled in someone else's country to know what's right!"

The embarrassment on his face made me shut up. Our neighbor, Mrs. Setney, Kristel—what did they know about wounded pride, about how it felt to be taken over by a foreigner, a foreigner ruling their land, their fate, to see their country exploited, crumble? What did they know about how it felt to be weak, powerless to stop one's freedom from being stolen?

⁂

The Palestinian pointed his rifle at my face.

"Your ID!"

I looked at the armed teenage boy who had stopped me as I was going home. He was younger than my students. But he was armed. I handed him my ID. However, I couldn't control my tongue.

"What gives you the right to demand an ID from a Lebanese when you're a Palestinian and a foreigner here?"

He gave me contemptuous stare but said nothing. Was it because I was a woman, because he didn't need to say anything with a gun in his hand?

⁂

"Your ID!"

I gave it to the Israeli soldier who had come into my home with two other soldiers.

"Palestinian?"

"Lebanese, but I was born in Palestine."

They went from room to room. They opened cupboards, emptied drawers, looked through photo albums.

"Where are all the pictures of the terrorists?"

I said nothing. They continued to search. They opened shoe boxes, suitcases, throwing everything to the floor.

"Where are the guns?"

I broke my silence.

"Do you really think that with all these books in the house, there are guns hidden here?"

He slapped me.

"Shut up!"

He slapped me again. His comrade intervened: "We're just following orders. We have orders to search for terrorists and their guns."

Rubbing my stinging cheek, I replied, "I'm the first to want to get rid of guns and armed men. Did you find any guns so you can hit me and insult me some more?"

However I realized what was behind the slaps and insults—I was Palestinian. It was politics taking an ironic jab at me and my allegiances!

❧

"Your ID!"

I handed it over to the Syrian soldier who had stopped my car on the corner just before my house. I passed by him four times a day, and every time he asked me for my ID, and every time he searched my car. They all asked me for my ID, and I was in my own country! But what were all these others doing in my country—Mrs. Setney, the Palestinian, the Israeli, the Syrian . . . The rifles in their hands dispensed with the need for questions from me, or an answer from them.

My country?

❧

I was watching the principal behind his large desk. While he read over my application, I was studying his expression. This school was near my house and I wanted to transfer to save time and the cost of travel. His face, however, was a mask. Eventually, he raised his head and looked at me.

"Are you Palestinian?"

"My father was Palestinian, my mother was Lebanese. After he died, she reassumed her nationality, and my sister and I took on her nationality."

It must have been to make sure I didn't need a work permit (I didn't know then that Palestinians didn't need a work permit in Lebanon).

"That's odd, there's nothing in your accent to suggest that you were originally from Palestine. How is that?"

I didn't miss the wariness in his eyes or voice, so I quickly replied with enthusiasm, "Because I have a Lebanese sensibility and my allegiance is to Lebanon. I feel that this is my country."

His sarcastic laughter cut right through me.

"That's what you all feel, to the good fortune of this country!"

My face blazed. Stupid woman! How could I expect him to believe me? He thought I was trying to flatter him to get the job. The derision in his tone rankled me.

"You didn't understand what I meant! I love Lebanon just like any loyal Lebanese loves his country. Surely there are Lebanese who identify with . . ."

". . . the Palestinian cause at the expense of Lebanese national interests?"

"Of course!"

I didn't get the job.

❧

"I'd like to introduce you to my colleague Saada Rayyis . . . Adel Jawhar, my nephew."

I shook the hand of the tall, slim young man whom Salwa had introduced me to. He had a brown complexion and a thick mustache which almost covered his thin lips. Was that a gleam of intelligence, energy, or curiosity in his young eyes? His conversation gave me the answer.

"Rayyis? Are you from Alay?"

I hesitated slightly. The image of the principal reading over my application came to mind. And this was before the war with the Palestinians in Lebanon!

"No. From Jerusalem."

Why did the Lebanese always ask where and what village a person came from? If I had been from Alay the question wouldn't have irritated me.

"My father was Palestinian and my mother was Lebanese," I added.

Did I say that so they would accept me as one of them, that I wasn't a foreigner? But I had learned I shouldn't talk about my feelings, my allegiances. Then the expected remark came.

"That's strange, but your accent doesn't betray where you come from."

The phrase "doesn't betray" really got under my skin. "Doesn't betray" meant that a person had something to hide. I didn't want to hide anything. I didn't boast about where I came from, nor did I want to hide it. Origin, identity, allegiance—words which for us had tragic connotations and dimensions. But what about for others? The French considered Napoleon a Frenchman although he was from Corsica. The Germans never mentioned that Hitler was an Austrian and thought of himself as one of them. But Napoleon and Hitler achieved greatness and power. And ordinary people? Adel's voice cut short my reflections.

"Salwa told me you're very fond of classical music. I have a large collection of Brahms records. Do you like him?"

Origin, identity, allegiance weren't a tragic problem to everyone, but then I was no Napoleon or Hitler.

"Yes, I do, very much so. But all I have is two or three myself."

"In that case, I'd like to invite you to come and listen to them at my place."

I accepted the invitation.

৯৯

Now politics had succeeded in sending Suha away from me. Politics and war—there was no great difference between them in Lebanon at the time. Suha was leaving in a month. Suha and Nadia and Anwar. They were the last and the dearest of all I had left. I watched the waves stretching out before me. An endless sea. An endless separation. An ocean would separate me from my sister. I would never see her. Nadia's laughter would never fill the emptiness of my life or banish my fears. Nadia would grow up, and I would never see her grow up. I wouldn't hear the stories about her teachers or classmates. She would never ask me about the meaning of an expression or the pronunciation of a word. Pronunciation? My language would disappear from her life—there would be no need for me to instruct her in pronunciation. She would change from a teenager into a young woman. To a woman, a wife, a mother. She would get married, and I wouldn't be at the wedding. She would become a mother, and I wouldn't know her children. Wasn't it enough for Suha to have been away from her country twice—in exile, really—without her wanting to leave again? Or was it an escape from one state of exile that was slowly eating into her to another that would leave her numb and make her forget? "Out of sight out of mind" as the saying goes—my proverbs again! I smiled to myself.

12

Packing. Phone calls. Cardboard boxes. Phone calls. Crates.

"In this box is the stuff I don't want. I'm giving it away to anyone who wants it."

Saada looked at the open box then at Suha. Didn't the thought of being apart bother her? Was she herself clinging to a dim and distant past, a past that had reached a dead end, perhaps, hardly noticing the more recent course of her life which was more alive, where she was getting by easily without her? She was the chameleon, which changed its color, but not its blood. She studied Suha's face as she took the clothes from the closet. Suha looked at a blouse and tossed it aside. A wrap she put in the suitcase at her feet without a second thought. She looked, deliberated, picked, and packed.

"You can't help me. You don't know what I want to take."

Saada went back to her chair, her thoughts, her silence, her intransigence. Activity filled Suha's hours. Now, her own hours—emptiness. And afterwards, would the emptiness grow, an emptiness left behind by Suha, Nadia? There would be no more spending the weekend with Suha, no more calling her every evening to tell her about what had happened that day, to listen to her news. There would be no Suha to show the new dress she had bought, to tell when she got a raise, the sister who knew there was no jealousy behind her sharing in her happiness, that there was no thought of revenge behind her wanting to support her in whatever she did. They would go away, and behind them would be left an emptiness of time and space as an eternal reminder of their presence . . . and absence. Suha's favorite chair would greet her with its emptiness whenever she looked at it. On the shelf, the cup with flowers on it, the only cup Nadia would drink from, would remind her that Nadia would never drink from it again. And Suha? The new, the different would fill her life. She would be busy getting used to everything—getting used to the weather in a foreign land, the strangeness of the people, the practices, the customs, the values. All of it strange, foreign. All the inhabitants would be strangers. Suha wouldn't feel that she alone was the stranger. Here the practices, the customs, the values told her she wasn't a stranger, but she was a stranger. And the language! The language in which she felt and thought, and dreamed as well, linking her to her past, to her roots. She wouldn't hear the words of this language, or its letters: the *Qaaf* which came from the depths of the throat, the depths of the heart; the *Daad* which proudly filled the mouth; the *Ayn* which moaned because it didn't want to be separated from its sisters, its land. The language! If she, Saada, had to speak all day in a language not her own, hour after hour, day after day, year after year, her tongue would become twisted and knotted. Her tongue, but not Suha's.

"What are you thinking about?"

Suha's question cut the thread of her thoughts. Saada looked up at her: "It bothers me I can't help out."

"Why don't you go to the kitchen and make Nadia's afternoon snack. She'll be here in a few minutes."

She welcomed anything that would distract her from her feelings and fears, so she went to the kitchen.

Suha sat on the end of the bed, staring at the open suitcase, staring but not seeing. *Saada will be alone. What if she has a relapse? But the doctor reassured us. Do we trust him or his statistics? Saada trusts him and trusts herself. She has always been like that—independent, arrogant, alone . . . Is she alone because she's so arrogant? She's been full of herself since she was little and no one likes her . . . maybe because she's so self-centered, so preoccupied with herself, her work, her plans, her profession? She hasn't been forced to make any sacrifices, for a husband or a child . . . Maybe she never got married because she's so self-centered? Sameer was interested in her: "He wasn't refined enough." Really! Basem liked her. She turned him down: "All he's interested in is money." As though someone who's only interested in money isn't good enough for her, the modest little teacher! And my life with Anwar—it isn't paradise, but it's better than being alone. And Nadia, my lovely Nadia! And is Anwar going to be successful?*

The doorbell snatched her from her thoughts. Nadia had come back from school. She went back to the closet, the boxes, the suitcases, the crates.

҉

The removal men took out the last crate and Suha let out a deep sigh: "Finally! . . . I called Anwar yesterday. I told him we were leaving at noon today."

"What about your belongings?"

"They'll arrive in a couple of months or so. The removal company is going to take care of shipping it. Anwar's rented a furnished apartment for the time being."

Saada looked at her watch.

"When are you leaving the house?"

"In about an hour. We're getting a taxi to the airport."

The sisters fell silent. Saada's gaze wandered over the empty room: "The house looks smaller without furniture."

The doorbell rang. Was she annoyed she wasn't going to be able to spend the last hour alone with her sister? Might she not welcome somebody to alleviate the heaviness of that last hour and the iciness she was feeling?

"Saada, I'd like to introduce you to the landlord's wife, Mrs. Lateef, and her daughters, Rita and Joyce. Sitt Najla, this is my sister . . . Here are the keys to the apartment."

She held out a key ring.

"Oh no, keep them until you leave. I'll get them from the concierge."

Suha smiled: "Unfortunately I don't have any chairs for you to sit down on."

Mrs. Lateef's hand was already on the door as she replied, "We only came to say good-bye, Sitt Suha. I'm sorry you're going, you've been a good neighbor. Is there anything we can do for you?"

"No, thank you."

The two girls started to leave, but their mother stayed where she was and asked, "Where's Nadia?"

This time Saada answered, "She's at the Sharar's, saying good-bye to their children."

"Fortunately today is Sunday, so she can see all her friends before she leaves," Suha said.

Najla Lateef turned to Saada: "Are you staying or are you also moving abroad?"

"I'm staying," was all Saada replied, her lips curled in a weak smile, so Suha added, "Saada is a teacher of Arabic literature at the high school. She could never do without her students or her language."

"Arabic literature?" Rita shot Saada a look of surprise, or did Saada imagine her lips twisted in contempt and disapproval? Then Rita said with pride, "I don't like Arabic."

Her sister pitched in, "What's the point of a language which is no good for commerce or economics or science or technology?"

Saada wanted to say, "Because scholars in economics and technology are what you are," but she said, "The modern Arab renaissance has come about due to the Lebanese, or rather the Christians and the Maronites—Bustani, Yazeeji, Shidyaq, Gibran, Rihani . . ."

Saada stopped talking. She realized from the backs turned to her that she was just boring them with names from a world they rejected. Rita and Joyce rejected them because although Christian they were Arab, and Ali had rejected her because although Arab she was Christian. Idealistic? Naive! She watched the three women as they embraced and kissed Suha. Then they shook Saada's hand and left. As soon as Suha closed the door behind them, the doorbell rang.

"Maybe you better leave the door open."

Other neighbors came from her building and the building next door. Saada stood in the corner, observing their comings and goings, their farewells, their conversations, their good wishes. How could Suha do without all this? How could she do without the human warmth, the like of which could be found nowhere else in the world? The hour flew by.

Now her turn came. A lump of overwhelming emotion in her throat choked her. Saada hugged and squeezed Nadia, burying her face in her hair and nuzzling her neck. Then Suha. Saada didn't look at her when they embraced. She held her tight for a minute or two. A choking, stifling silence rose between the sisters. Without either uttering a single word they drew apart. Then, without looking at her sister, Saada rushed out of the house and down the stairs to the street outside. As she walked along, she could still feel her sister's body trembling against hers. She quickened her pace, urged on by her sister's awful silence until she reached the corner. She turned around and saw Suha waving at her from the balcony. Nadia was at her side waving a white handkerchief so her aunt would see her. Saada waved back once or twice. As she rounded the corner, they disappeared from sight; then she broke down in tears.

৵৽

Saada gazed at their heads bent over their books, looking from one to the other. Jihad, as usual, was mouthing the words while he followed Lamia's recitationl. How she had tried to stop that habit of his. She smiled. And Nabeel, poor Nabeel, whom nature had granted nothing: he wasn't intelligent, good-looking, and he didn't even have a sense of humor. Nothing. Sameer was the lucky one. If only he wasn't so conceited and full of himself. That was the difference between him and Hana. Hana was intelligent, pretty, and sweet natured. Saada interrupted her musings to listen to Lamia:

> Our enemies, enraged that we did drink the cup of love
> prayed it's drought be bitter. Fate said: So be it.
> Thus between our souls the cord was cut,
> the close congress of our hands was severed.
> In former days, no fear that we would part,
> but now, no hope that we should meet.

The Andalusian poet is speaking to me. I never once imagined Suha and I would be apart, that I wouldn't see her, be near her when I needed her . . . The terrible loneliness . . . Ibn Zaydoun was forced to part from Willaada by his enemies and those who were jealous of him. And me, who took Suha away from me? Enemies, friends? I cannot tell who is the enemy and who is the friend anymore. Enemy, friend, loyalist, traitor. My homeland, lackey. Words mean one thing to me and the opposite to someone else. But not these words on their own. Language again! Are there words in languages besides Arabic which mean one thing and the opposite? "Rubba," "many" or "not a great many"; "Mawla," which could mean "master" or "slave"; "Waahi," which could mean "weak" or "strong." Hundreds of words, used by poets and bellettrists, classified and defined by scholars. Perhaps it's because these words came from the tongues of ancient tribes, and every tribe had its own expressions. And today? Are we tribes?

৵

The armed youth took me to his party HQ and handed me over to his commander.

"Please, sit down."

I sat down. Between the commander and me was a large desk. On the wall behind him were pictures of his own leaders: the ideologues, Lebanese and non-Lebanese. He pulled out a drawer, took out a notebook, and opened it.

"Your ID!" he demanded in a harsh tone.

I gave it to him and said, "I'm Lebanese like you."

Let him think me simple-minded. He looked at my ID and noted the details in his book.

"Don't worry. We've stopped a lot of Christians, and we haven't hurt any."

"Why did you stop me? What did I do?"

He stopped writing and looked up at me angrily.

"Do? You tried to get away when my men went up to your car!"

His tone made me really angry.

"Get away? Would you let some strange men go up to your sister or your wife if they were in a car?"

"They were trying to search it. We received information it had been booby-trapped."

"They never told me that. I thought they were trying to steal it, and I need it to get to my job!"

Was it my imagination or did the anger in his eyes vanish when he asked, "Your job? What do you do?"

"I teach . . . at the high school."

"I have some nephews and nieces at that school. What do you teach?"

No, I wasn't dreaming—his tone had changed, its harshness had gone.

"Arabic language and literature," I said with pride.

He looked at me as if suspicious or wary and asked, "Who are your favorite poets?" He was testing me.

"Sayyab, Khalil Hawi, Adonis," I told him in all sincerity.

A wide smile covered his face: "So, you're a patriot?"

His remark provoked me, so I replied without a moment's

thought, "A patriot? Does being a patriot depend whether you're a certain religion, faction, or ideology?"

He didn't reply, but returned my ID, then walked me out to my car and sent me on my way. What would have happened to me if I had been a French Christian or a Yemeni Muslim, for example? I could imagine the sense of well-being enjoyed by those who belonged to the majority in a country, the feeling of security enjoyed by those who weren't contending with a tangle of allegiances to different or warring groups. I had been rejected by every group because every group only accepted allegiance to itself and no other, without recognizing the possibility of a loyalty that rejected this contention by embracing the differences. Idealistic, perhaps, but this didn't rid me of my pain or feelings of loss. I smiled to myself. Wasn't it strange that someone who maintained all these allegiances could feel loss?

I thought again about language and words. Patriotism had a nationalistic connotation for me and a religious connotation for others. Treason to me meant betraying your own country or nation. To others it meant betraying the president or leader even if he was from another country or nation. Nationalism for me was in my culture, my language, my heritage. And other people? They might ridicule me and my language, culture, and heritage. I, you, they . . . Who was right? I remember Gibran in *Storms:* "Among the petals of a rose and its thorns sleeps the truth in deep eternal slumber."

෴

Through the mists of memory Saada felt something was different. Silence was knocking at the door of her consciousness. Thirty pairs of puzzled and curious eyes were staring at her. They shook her from her thoughts and memories, and she said, "How does Ibn Zaydoun differentiate his past from his present?"

Hands went up, and their answers brought her back to the present and back to them.

13

The waiting room was full. The hands of the clock on the wall were pointing to five. Her appointment had been for half-past three! The door to the clinic had not opened once since she had been there. "Please, make yourself comfortable," the receptionist had said when Saada had told her her name and that she had an appointment with Doctor Labeeb. She had sat down and made herself comfortable . . . She went over in her mind for the hundredth time the letter her sister had written to her. She knew the letter by heart she had read it so often: "I'm not thinking about Nadia or the days to come. In my mind is this image of you running off as we were saying our good-byes. You turned your back on our parting, turned your back on me. That's all I saw, your back. You were angry at me for leaving, angry that you had somehow failed. When the stewardess shut the airplane door, It wasn't that she was shutting you out, but shutting me out, closing the door on a life, severing me from a past. I cried. I cried until I could cry no more. I never knew I could cry so much. I cried until my tears dried up."

For an hour and a half all had been quiet when Saada noticed a man suddenly stand up, walk up to the receptionist, and shout in her face, "One hour I've been waiting! I've never know such lack of respect for people or their time!"

The young woman's face turned red, but she replied calmly, "I'm sorry, Sir. The doctor is still in the operating theater."

A woman spoke up: "Why does he make appointments on the days he's operating?"

"So he doesn't lose a penny of profit!" someone answered sarcastically.

The receptionist said, "He had to fill in for a doctor who is absent and the operation is urgent."

The waiting room became silent once more. Saada cleared her throat and said, "Did he say when he's coming?"

Before the receptionist could reply the telephone rang. Everyone's eyes turned to her as she said, "Okay . . . Yes."

She threw a quick glance over the appointments book in front of her: "Ten, Doctor . . . Fine."

As she hung up, their eyes remained fixed on her.

"The doctor will be here in half an hour or so. For those who can't wait, I'll make another appointment."

"What, so I can lose another day? I'll wait, thank you."

The angry man again. Six people went up to the receptionist to reschedule their appointments. Saada remained with the others.

Suha hadn't told her about her new house or the people she had met. She had only told her that Nadia was going to school and was quickly settling in. And Suha? If she were settling in, her letter would have been different. If she couldn't settle in here, how could she settle in there?

Then she heard the receptionist say, "Saada Rayyis. Please go through."

⁓

Saada gave him the sealed envelope which she had picked up from the laboratory the day before. He opened it and asked her, "How do you feel?"

"I get tired quickly, Doctor. For me that's unusual."

He unfolded the sheets of paper and, without looking at her, said, "Don't forget the operation was only four months ago. And you really need to rest more before you go back to work."

He started to read the laboratory report. Her eyes never left his face.

"Everything seems normal. Please go through so I can examine you."

They went into the next room. She took off her clothes and put on the white gown the nurse had handed to her. She lay down on the examination table but was wracked by a sudden fit of coughing, so she sat up then lay down again. The doctor came in and leaned over her, pressing her abdomen and lower abdomen with his fingers. He picked up his stethoscope and moved it over her back and her scarred chest, pausing briefly to listen to her breathing. Had he discovered anything? She coughed slightly.

"Are you sure you don't feel anything?"

The doctor stood upright and fixed her with a serious stare.

"I have difficulty breathing sometimes . . . It's because I'm tired."

"What about the cough?"

"It's only a very slight cough, doctor. It doesn't bother me."

The doctor didn't comment and only said, "Get dressed please."

He left the room. When she went into his office, he was folding a sheet of paper. He placed it in an envelope and handed it to her.

"Miss Saada, I'd like you to get your lungs X-rayed. These are specifications for the type of X-ray I need."

"Is the disease spreading?"

(How do you say the word "cancer"?) She couldn't speak or get her hand to move out of fear. She just stared into the doctor's eyes. After what seemed like an eternity, he said, "We hope it isn't . . . I'm not too happy with that cough of yours."

"But it's only very slight!"

Maybe it was only slight, or maybe she didn't have the courage to face being sick again and having another operation. When her breast had been removed, they had told her, "Eighty percent of cancer cases recover." But was she in the remaining 20 percent? The doctor hadn't seen the need for chemotherapy, but was that because the disease was spreading, because she was in the 20 percent? Percentages. To them, numbers, abstractions. She was a human being, and 20 percent of people were not just numbers.

Saada took the envelope and left. This time she was going to be on her own. Suha wasn't going to be there when she had her chest X-rayed, or be with her for the results of the X-ray, or when she made another appointment, or as she was sitting in the doctor's office waiting for the verdict. Was she in the 80 percent, the 20 percent? Would she have to go back to the hospital and have another operation? Would it do her any better than the first? . . . The thirst as she came out of the anesthetic, and they wouldn't give her anything to drink. The pain of the surgery, the endless hours of night, the pain as soon as she woke up, and the intravenous drips stuck in her hand. She had had to sleep on her side, but she couldn't get used to it. The daylight hours crawled by monotonously, emptily. The white walls of the room revived her memories of the past. Or was it her fear of death?

She could refuse the operation, but the doctor wouldn't be happy. He would give her more statistics, more examples of someone having a lung removed and living for twenty years, and someone else living for seven years on just one lung. But what about the ones who died? Numbers. Percentages. Numbers in a book.

She walked on and on. The stores were closed. The streets were empty. She had to get back . . .

She shut the door behind her and sat in the darkness. Maybe she should write to Suha or Anwar. What was the use, thousands of miles separated them. She was how old, and she didn't have a single friend to tell her fears to, to comfort her. She had acquaintances, colleagues, but not a single friend. She just had Suha and Anwar. And now?

She felt cold. She turned on the lights and went to the closet to get a cardigan. Just because Kristel, Amer, and Ali had betrayed her maybe she was afraid of being betrayed again. And what about herself? Najla had liked her, and she had wounded her. Sumayya had stood by her, and she had insulted her. Conceited, arrogant—that was what everybody else had said about her. If only they knew what was behind the mask. Now she was paying the price: standing alone, assuming the burden of her sickness, fears, and loneliness.

৵৽

The receptionist gave her a large sealed envelope. Saada studied her expression—nothing. Maybe she should ask, but what was the use—she was only the receptionist. Tomorrow the doctor would tell her . . .

Their heads were bent over their exercise books. She didn't feel strong enough to teach them something new. She didn't feel up to grading their essays, dozens and dozens of pages: content, organization of ideas, grammar. She walked down the rows where their hands were writing away. She could put off grading to . . . What would he see in the X-ray?

"Miss, where do you write the *hamza* on *Jaru*?"

Nabeel and his stupid questions, the idiot!

"How many times have I explained the rules of the *hamza!* Think before you ask!"

What was the point of thinking about it? The result was in the X-ray, in her lung. The thread of her destiny remained for her to discover . . . The bell—two more hours and she could go home. Even Nabeel's questions were better than the cold hard walls, the empty chairs, the absolute silence.

She fled to the movie theater. Color images flickered across the screen. She looked at them and forgot the intransigence of her life. She listened to the music, the actors speaking. She didn't understand what they were saying, but their voices dispelled the silence, filled the emptiness. Movement, voices, noise. People living their lives, talking, walking, laughing. And between them and her, a wall of her fear and loneliness.

She had to go back home. She went in the door, and before even taking off her coat, she turned on the record player. Mozart, maybe? She picked out *Tanhauser*. Only the tumultuous music of Wagner could possibly chase away the heavy silence.

The day dragged on, as though the minutes were frozen in time.

๛

Saada didn't have to wait. As soon as she arrived at the clinic, the receptionist told her to go in. A good omen, or had the doctor found out something that needed to be dealt with in a hurry?

Her hand wouldn't stop shaking as she gave the doctor the large brown envelope. He opened it as he walked over to a machine that looked like a closet in the corner of the room. She didn't take her eyes off him as he placed an X-ray on the screen. He turned on the light and examined it. Did the small gray shadows mean anything? The doctor turned his back to her. She couldn't read his expression. A second X-ray replaced the first. Minutes later, a third. He turned off the light and took off the X-ray. She was afraid to look at his face now. Let her have one more minute of ignorance and hope. She looked down, her eyes tracing the green zig-zag on the brown carpet. How ugly!

"Miss Saada."

Her heart was pounding. She forced herself look at his lips and eyes—a mask. To him, it was just like any other time. To her, her whole life was hanging by what she saw in his eyes.

"In one of the X-rays . . ."

Another operation? A lingering death? His voice cut through her wall of fear: "There's a small spot on the right lung . . . No call for alarm. The other lung is healthy, completely clear. We'll remove the tumor and at worst the lung. The tumor may not be malignant. Unfortunately, we won't know until we analyze it. But operations to remove lungs . . ."

His voice trailed off. So she knew. What if they were successful in 90, 95, or even 99 percent of cases, there was still the 1 percent, and this 1 percent might be her, a human being who had her family, her loved ones, her work, her activities, her hobbies, her plans, her hopes, her life.

"Did you hear me, Miss Saada? You will have to make a quick decision so I can book a room in the hospital. The sooner you're operated on the better."

As if in a dream or a nightmare, she nodded her head, got up, walked toward the door, opened it, closed it, descended the stairs, and went out into the street.

The decision once again, and again would it change anything? They had removed her breast: 80 percent of breast cancer cases recovered.

But wait, might not she be in the remaining 20 percent—would removing the lung prevent her from being included in the 10 percent which couldn't be cured? Statistics, numbers, percentages, and lost among them were human beings. What if she decided not to have the operation and save the expense, doing away with all those monotonous and painful days and nights in hospital, doing away with the hope that she was in the 90 percent?

She arrived home. What should she do; whom should she ask for advice? The decision was hers alone: the doctor's diagnosis, his opinion was clear. But what about her opinion? She glanced at her watch. She had to tell Suha, but it was 10:00 A.M. in Montreal, and she wouldn't be at home. She would have to wait until tomorrow. But would tomorrow come? What would it bring?

She sat in her office, the stack of essays in front of her. She turned over the pages—Sameer's essay, she would start with Sameer's essay. It would encourage her to grade the rest. "Mutanabbi succeeded in producing a new image . . ." There was a spot in the X-ray—a malignant or benign tumor maybe? "We won't know until we remove it." What if it's a relapse? ". . . in producing a new image from that of the old . . ." "The new surgical techniques can work miracles," the doctor had told her. The latest advances in medical science, surgery. The mastectomy had been successful; the breast had been removed, but the tumor, the tumor had appeared in another place. That would be removed. Surgery could remove anything . . . except fear . . . and death.

She tossed the essays aside. Among them and Mutanabbi's images was another image—life, her life. She paced the room back and forth. She peered through the window—the streets were empty. She started pacing around the room again, counting her steps: ten steps there, ten steps back. She walked across the room a third time then a fourth, counting . . . eighty-eight, eighty-nine.

The ringing of the telephone interrupted the tedium of her counting, lifted the weight of her loneliness.

"Hello?"

"I have a call from Canada, please hold the line."

Her heart began to beat faster. How could she know? Did she know? She heard Suha say, "Saada, how are things with you?"

Should she tell her or not?

"Saada, can you hear me?"

Saada paused then asked, "Why are you calling? Is there anything wrong?"

A few seconds silence followed then Suha answered, "No, we're fine. I don't know why, but I woke up feeling worried. Just some kind of premonition about you. How are you?"

Should she risk it and tell her. How often had she scoffed at people who believed in things like that, and here was her sister on the line.

"I was at Doctor Labeeb's this afternoon."

She fell silent. Then she heard her sister asking anxiously, "Saada, are you feeling okay?"

The alarm in Suha's voice shook her. How could she tell her?

"He discovered a small spot on the right lung. The tumor may not be malignant. He wants to remove the tumor so he can analyze it."

"And the lung?" Suha shrieked.

Saada tried to keep her voice calm and steady as she replied, "Having a lung removed is not the end of the world. Thousands of people live with only one lung. My other lung is completely healthy, thank God."

She didn't feel as worried as before. True, why might not she be one of those thousands? Suha's question again interrupted the thread of her thoughts: "When are you going to have the operation? You shouldn't be on your own."

"As soon as possible. I have to decide so the doctor can book a room in the hospital."

"Absolutely not. Come over here, Saada. You can go to the hospital here. Anwar can advise you."

Dear sweet rash Suha. Saada smiled to herself.

"What about the visa, Suha? Have you forgotten the Canadian embassy in Beirut is closed? I would have to travel to Syria to get one, and they might refuse my application. And then there's the cost of travel and the hospital . . . and the time. The doctor wants to perform the operation as soon as possible."

Saada fell silent, Suha fell silent. Then Suha said, "I'll ask Anwar, I'll get his advice. I'll call you tomorrow. Don't make a decision before tomorrow, Saada."

The line went dead.

Saada stayed in her chair. *I'm not jealous or envious of her. I can't believe how better off I am. When Suha gets flustered, she goes to Anwar for advice. When Suha doesn't know something, she asks Anwar. She trusts completely that Anwar will give her the right advice, the right answer. If he's so dedicated to his profession, why doesn't he care how empty her life is or care about her feelings? But, he did come back to Beirut with her because she wanted to. He went to Canada for her sake. He has always stood by her—reliable, trustworthy, loyal—a pillar of strength for her. And me? Strong, independent!* Her lips curled into a derisive smile . . . *Boyfriends? "Don't eat all of your beloved even if he's made of honey." You have a boyfriend, and he's with you for an hour, a day, not the whole of your life. He has his concerns, his goals, his aims, his personal well-being, like me, but they're not my concerns, my goals, my aims, my personal well-being. Suha's well-being is Anwar's, her concerns his. My life—what have I done with it? A successful teacher! In my loneliness all I have are my students' essays to comfort me. In my confusion and fear all I have to comfort me are these dull, mediocre essays: "Renewal in Mutanabbi's Images." What great comfort and consolation! I'm successful—compared to whom? My students? They will become doctors and engineers, office workers, journalists and businessmen, husbands and wives, fathers and mothers, and they will remember nothing of Tarafa and Mutanabbi except what might help them explain a qasida to their children.*

She smiled scornfully to herself. Wasn't that success enough? She smiled scornfully again as she got up to go to the kitchen to make a cup of tea.

Tomorrow she would phone Suha. *Suha will give me Anwar's answer. Will he tell Ali? Will Ali come to visit me again? If he had been true to me, I*

wouldn't have needed anyone else! "Don't hate something—it might be good
for you," was what Papa always said. Might it be true of Ali? Perhaps, but that's
something I'll never know. What about other men? "You're so conceited, you're
so difficult," Suha told me repeatedly, because I turned down men I didn't
respect or love.

"As many loves your heart will chance . . ." "Your true love is your first love
. . ." Is that what it is? Suha loved Mounir then Anwar, and Naeema loved
Saad then married Anis . . . Is it because I'm romantic, because of the poetry I
love and which deceives me, good luck, or just me, Saada the monkey? . . . "She
won't need a husband to provide for her," Mama said. Why didn't it occur to
her I might just need support, not a provider? Tomorrow she would phone Suha.

She carried the cup of tea to bed.

14

She sat in the chair, staring at the bare white wall in front of
her. Back in the hospital, all on her own this time. Suha wouldn't get
there for another two days. Would she? . . .

৯

There was a gentle knock on the door.

"Come in."

The door opened to reveal the face of a young woman in her thirties
with a pale wide face and large brown eyes. Saada noticed the eyes
above all else, drawn to their light-hearted smile.

"Miss Saada, do you remember me?"

The woman walked into the room. She was of average height and
slightly plump. She was wearing a white gown. A nurse? There was
nothing on her head to suggest that. Saada searched her memory.

"My name's Zaynab Maysour."

The name meant nothing to her, and the soft voice continued: "I
was a student of yours back in . . . back in . . ."

She laughed.

"Can you believe it, Miss? I've forgotten how many years it's been. I graduated from the school of medicine, and I'm now in gynecology."

Suddenly Saada remembered: the smile in her large brown eyes when she reprimanded her for having forgotten her homework, the smile when she punished her for not having done her homework or learned the poem. Always that smile. How it irritated her—such a nonchalant smile. Neither persuasion, nor reprimand, nor threat had any effect on her. And here she was now, a doctor!

"You have every right to have forgotten me, Miss. I was a lazy and inattentive student."

Saada smiled: "No, I haven't forgotten you. But it looks like you've changed. You didn't stay lazy."

Zaynab said with a measure of enthusiasm, "It's because I could study what I liked. I had always dreamed of being a doctor since I was little, and I didn't like literature."

Thoughts flashed through Saada's mind: *If I had been like you, my mother's dreams would have been realized. And literature is only useful for helping you explain a qasida by Tarafa or Mutanabbi to your children.*

"How did you know I was here?"

Zaynab smiled and said, "It's my particular field. I've been keeping count of the operations performed on women here for the last six months to assess the number of breast, womb, and ovarian cancer cases, and I came across your name. I called Doctor Labeeb, but you had already left the hospital, but then he informed me you were back in."

She fell silent. An awkward silence filled the room, then Saada said wearily, "Unfortunately, your statistics aren't much help."

Embarrassed, Zaynab looked away from the face of her teacher to the floor. They had respected her, even those who didn't like her. She was sincere, fair, energetic, strong. They were afraid of her because she was strict, stern. To them, she was an abstract image, a teacher, and it never once occurred to them that she was a human being. In her mind was this image of herself as a teacher, and it had changed into a human being, a worried, weak, sick human being.

"Please take a seat, Zaynab."

Zaynab looked up to see a smile on the face of the old woman. No, the image had lost none of its sternness or force.

"I'm sorry, Miss, I have to go back to work, but I'll come back and spend some time with you when I get off. When is the operation?"

Zaynab's reply stung her. How stupid of her! Why hadn't she realized that the girl might have more to do than just visit an old sick teacher?

"Tomorrow morning, at eight."

Zaynab's eyes smiled their eternal smile.

"Good, the first thing you'll see is your lazy, inattentive student." She laughed and left the room.

"What made her want to stay with me?" Saada wondered, and she got up to tidy her belongings.

⁂

In post-op Saada had a raging thirst, and her mouth was dry. Her tongue was stuck to the back of her throat. She turned her head and opened her eyes then closed them. She wanted a drink of water. Her mouth was so dry that she couldn't speak. She opened her eyes again . . . This wasn't Suha by her. A thick fog shrouded her mind, and she closed her eyes. Who was by her? She lapsed into unconsciousness. A half-hour later she opened her eyes again to see somebody leaning over her. Who was it? As a sweet smile pierced the fog she suddenly remembered. She heard a pleasant-sounding voice say, "Praise be to God for your well-being, Miss."

The smile spread from her eyes to her whole face. Saada gathered her strength to part her lips and move her tongue which felt like wood.

"Water."

That was the only word that came out. Zaynab leaned over and gently stroked her hand.

"Be patient a while longer. We can't give you anything to drink just yet."

Saada's eyes fluttered and closed as the voice said, "I'm happy to say, Miss, that . . ."

The rest of the sentence was lost in the fog of unconsciousness. When Saada woke up, she was back in her room. Once again the intravenous tubes, the bags of saline solution, and in front of her . . .

"Samiya?" Saada asked hesitantly in a barely-audible whisper.

The girl got up from her chair and approached the bed.

"Do you remember me, Miss?"

⁓

"I've never known a class whose grammar is so weak!"

I handed them back the essays that I had graded the evening before, and said, my voice raised on a note of anger and despair, "I ask myself what is the use in trying to do poetry explication with you when you don't even know the active from the passive!"

Complete silence. I continued: "I'm going to ask the principal to let me drop literature and teach you the basics of grammar."

A girl raised a hand. No doubt she was going to argue that literature was on the high school curriculum, that if they flunked Arabic literature they could make up for it by doing well in other subjects, and all that mattered to them was getting a high school diploma, not writing good Arabic or learning to appreciate Hafez or Ibn Rumi. That I was furious was clear in the way I said, "Yes?"

I saw she was hesitant, so I asked, "What's your name?"

"Samiya Shakir."

The girl paused, took a deep breath as though preparing to do battle with me, then said, "Miss, we know that our Arabic is weak and that we've been studying it for twelve years without it doing us much good."

I interrupted her sharply: "So, we can do without it then?"

Samiya said calmly, "Perhaps if we study the literature it will help our Arabic. Can we give it a try?"

Thirty pairs of hopeful eyes waited for me to speak, to decide. I thought, "If they have spent twelve years studying the language without it doing them much good, how would one year of literature help?" Ignorant teenagers, and how deluded! But their expectant eyes never left my face in an attempt to win my sympathy and favor. "Why not try?" I thought. "What do I have to lose? Literature is language, a language of beauty. If they love literature, they might love its language. Is not love the first step to knowledge?" So I said, "We'll give it a try."

An air of relief dispelled the tension, and I could sense the weight lifting from their frail shoulders. Of course, all they were worried about was passing the exams for the high school diploma.

We started studying literature, and their work actually improved. Maybe they felt it was a challenge or they wanted to prove they were right, or maybe because they were drawn to literature, they were drawn to language as well? The biggest surprise was Samiya, the weakest student in the class. No sooner had half of the academic year gone by than I began to wait impatiently for her papers, not to grade them, but to look forward to them for their sensitive analysis, their original criticism, their style—even their style. It was as if she had unconsciously assimilated the styles of our greatest poets whose works she had been inspired to write her papers on. That year I learned as much from my students as I myself taught them. I learned how ignorant I was about teaching methods despite my experience, and, more importantly, that the best and most successful teachers, without doubt, are the great poets and bellettrists.

ॐ

Did she remember her? "What brought you?" Saada asked out of curiosity.

Samiya leaned over her teacher so Saada could see her better, and replied, "Zaynab told me you were here . . . and that you were all alone. Do you need anything?"

Her chest hurt her, breathing hurt her, but she said, "Your being here is all I need."

She closed her eyes. Saada didn't see Samiya's lips trembling as she said, "It's the least we can do to return the favor, Miss."

Favor? Her duty. But could that restore her lung or her health? Samiya's voice pierced her apprehension: "We're pleased how the operation went."

The healthy making fun of the sick! She opened her eyes and said, "What, that I have one lung instead of two?"

Saada immediately regretted what she had said. It wasn't Samiya's fault. The girl wasn't making fun of her—she was trying to comfort her and didn't know how. Her vicious tongue, it had driven her colleagues away from her!

Looking at the smiling face above her, Saada quickly added, "Yes, thank God the other lung is healthy."

But why was Samiya smiling so broadly? She heard the answer to her silent question: "Don't you know? Didn't Zaynab tell you?"

Saada stared back into the smiling eyes.

"Tell me what?"

Samiya laughed, "Tell you that your lung wasn't removed!"

Were they lying about it, laughing about it to try to cheer her up? She didn't need this kind of thing. She heard the girl say, "The spot was a growth on the outside of the lung. Of course, they analyzed the growth, a routine analysis. The doctor is certain it's not malignant."

Was she hearing right? Was she dreaming? Was she just wishing for it to come true? She moved around in her bed. Samiya was right there before her, so she wasn't dreaming.

"Who told me that? When?" she asked hesitantly.

Still smiling, Samiya answered, "The doctor, Zaynab. She told you as soon as you regained consciousness and opened your eyes after the operation."

A tremendous joy rose from inside her, washing over her, putting her at rest. It had been her old students who had told her the good news. She would tell Suha the good news . . . tomorrow . . . the day after tomorrow . . . She closed her eyes and sank into a deep sleep.